# Just My Imagination

### Running Away With Me

## SHORT STORIES. ESSAYS. POEMS.

## JAMES L. THOMPSON, JR.

JUST MY IMAGINATION RUNNING AWAY WITH ME

ISBN: 979-8-9877718-0-8

# TABLE OF CONTENTS

## ESSAYS

## SHORT STORIES (1,000 WORDS OR LESS)

# POETRY

# LONG SHORT STORIES (1,000 WORDS OR MORE)

# FOREWORD

Funny, but I first met James Thompson after I had moved away from the city he lived in, which was in southeast Alabama. We'd met through a mutual colleague (a photographer) and from that phone call, he was inspired to send me his first two books, *Paper Orphans and Other Illegitimate Verse* and *Adopted for Publication*.

What first struck me was his wordsmithery. James not only has a way with language, but he plays with it, stretches it, molds it to humorous effect or to shock, surprise, or challenge the reader. He nails dialogue, renders character traits with a surgeon's precision, and gives you the vibe of a place all very naturally.

In this compilation of short stories, essays, and poetry, James touches on the light and easy topics like falling in love, first kisses, the doo-wop scene, and scary campfire stories, but also goes deep into difficult areas like race relations, human trafficking, and the divisiveness of politics. Never one to shy away from a full-on description no matter where it leads him or the reader, he is a chronicler and journalist as much as an artist and poet. It takes skill to pull this off. You won't be disappointed.

– Debbie Burke, author of *Death by Saxophone*

# FROM THE AUTHOR

My new book is not intended to be a scholarly work of art and may not win any awards, but it was very therapeutic and fun for me to compose. It felt like a literary exorcism to expose some of my dreams and nightmares and to expel all of the wicked demons and friendly ghosts that have haunted me for years. Sometimes, I don't sleep well, and I am awakened in the middle of the night by a thought, an idea, a word, a phrase, a poem, a song... that sets my imagination into motion and causes me to arise and record these muses. In full disclosure, three essays, three poems, and two long short stories are reprints herein from my two earlier books that are out of print now.

All writers seek inspiration from muses to help them create their works; my muses are my birthplace and my rich heritage of family and friends. This book is a love letter to them. Many of the stories in this book germinated from my feelings, experiences, and memories of Wakanda Dothan, Alabama, the cradle of my birth. I will forever be beholden to everyone who planted a seed in my mind and taught me how to cultivate my ideas like a literary plant farmer. I have made my living from my thoughts and actions, not by what I have built with my own hands. My father worked in construction and was a constructor of buildings. I have worked in education and justice and am a constructor of words and ideas that will hopefully outlive the buildings constructed by builders.

As a beginning writer in 1970, I worked hard to find my own voice. I read the writings of others and tried to emulate their successes with words but found that was not to be my reality. In order to find my own unique voice, I had to first realize that it was always there but needed to be customized to my own experiences and lifestyle. After years of being someone I described as a closet writer, I emerged from the closet with a new self-esteem based on the confidence that others and I placed in my writings. I deemed my style to be something I refer to as "SHACKOLOGY" – patterned after my nickname, Shack. (The origin of the nickname can be found within this book.)

So, to those of you who thought you knew me and those who don't, I, James L. "Shack" Thompson, Jr., dedicate this book to you and introduce you to new creative ideas from an undeniable power source: It's Just My Imagination Running Away with Me.

> "The power of imagination created the illusion that my vision went much farther than the naked eye could actually see."
> — Nelson Mandela (1918-2013)

> *I was not born with a silver spoon in my mouth,*
> *Not voted most likely to succeed;*
> *I was born in the dirty, dusty South,*
> *From my parents who planted my black seed.*
> *Through trial and error and hits and misses,*
> *I discovered a pathway to escape;*
> *Education showed me the way with lots of kisses,*
> *But most importantly, I was transformed from a raisin into a grape.*
> — James L. Thompson, Jr. (2023)

# Essays

*"If you fall in love with the imagination,*
*you understand that it is a free spirit.*
*It will go anywhere, and it can do anything."*
– Alice Walker (1944-present)

# FROM BAPTIST BOTTOM TO
# WAKANDA DOTHAN

In a world where it's easy to chemically alter your fingerprints, digitally Photoshop your images, and medically change your gender, it is almost impossible to change your DNA and your native heritage.

I was born in the Baptist Bottom in Dothan, Alabama.

Dothan is known as the Circle City because most of its citizenry lives inside the fourteen-mile circumference called the Ross Clark Circle. But the Baptist Bottom was like a city within the city with a wealth of history that belongs to all of the citizens regardless of race.

Tulsa had Black Wall Street. New York had Harlem. And Dothan had the Baptist Bottom that only encompassed a half-mile radius from the 1920s to the 1980s.

I grew up in a place that served a traditional Southern breakfast of grits, eggs, bacon, biscuits with syrup, milk, and coffee every morning. If we had orange juice, it came fresh from a can. Fridays were reserved for fried fish, and Sundays meant fried chicken and sweet tea with collard greens, cornbread, mashed potatoes, potato salad, and green beans. Sometimes we also had hot dogs, hamburgers, sloppy Joes, pork chops, chitterlings, pigs' feet, ribs, oxtails, and raw oysters. Kool-Aid, soft drinks, lemonade, sweet tea, and Tang were our "go-to" drinks. Words like cholesterol, hypertension, and diabetes were foreign to us, but some of the grown folks often talked about having "sugar" and high blood pressure.

What was the "Bottom," you may ask? Most people's connotation of the Bottom in any poverty-stricken locale is that it refers to a ghetto-like community where only low-income people reside. Not to be confused with Lincoln's Gettysburg Address, but everyone in the Bottom had a *ghettosburg* address.

Contrary to popular belief, the people who lived in the *Bottom* saw our neighborhood as a literal blue-collar Garden of Eden with a wellspring of co-existing Black-owned businesses including store owners, barber shops, hair salons, taxi drivers, dry cleaners, cafés, a hotel, preachers, poets, writers, funeral homes, musicians, singers, dancers, teachers, accountants, brick masons, home builders, mechanics, and numerous other trades and talents.

The George W. Carver movie theater was located in the Bottom, although it was not Black-owned. The Carver Theater was owned by Mr. Rufus Davis and family that had a reputation for fairness and respect for Blacks. The building was later acquired by the Bottom and repurposed for another use; the Davis family actually donated the building to the Bottom.

Inside the Bottom locale, there were plentiful flower gardens, pecan trees, and homegrown gardens with vegetables and fruits like corn, collards, turnips, squash, okra, peas, peppers, tomatoes, cucumbers, wild blackberries, mulberries, plums, peaches, apples, pomegranates, muscadines, figs, and even one banana tree. We seldom had to buy fruits and vegetables from a store.

Although we had an occasional shooting, stabbing, or killing in the Bottom, Black-on-Black crime was virtually minimal. We did not have to step over corpses daily to walk down the street. We said our prayers every night, but we never locked our doors. There were no wholesale kidnappings, robberies, bullying, rapes, or thefts, for the most part. It was a safe place to live for the inhabitants of our community because everyone knew everyone else. Neighbors had the express permission to discipline others' children if they saw those children committing wrongdoings, and the wrongdoers were disciplined by their parents again when they got home.

The moniker "Baptist Bottom" was coined because of the nearby large, red-bricked First Baptist Church. It was jokingly referred to as the *Bigshot Church* because most of the respectable and well-to-do Black people attended First Baptist; my family attended North Highland Baptist Church, a few blocks away.

One of the more famous preachers associated with First Baptist was the Rev. Howard Creecy, Sr., a tall, light-complexioned, handsome man that might remind one of Harlem's Adam Clayton Powell, Jr., another famous preacher and politician. The Rev. Creecy was well loved and he preached from the heart and soul to a community that rewarded him with their faithful attendance and tithes when they could afford to pay. In the 1960s, the customary weekly tithing for adults was $1 and for children it was twenty-five cents. We were taught that it is better to give than to receive at a young age, although I have to admit that I sometimes kept my quarter and used it to go to the movies on Sundays after church.

Another great preacher from First Baptist was the Rev. Rochester Johnson, Sr. If Rev. Creecy reminded one of Adam Clayton Powell, then the Rev. Johnson would remind them of the Rev. Dr. Martin Luther King, Jr. The Rev. Johnson was similar in height and skin complexion, and he preached with the same fiery cadence as Dr. King. He was a mighty man of God in the community that he proudly embraced as the Baptist Bottom.

Right behind First Baptist Church was the McRae Homes Housing Project that housed many of my childhood friends. We lived in a small shotgun house right across the street from the McRae Homes, but I spent so much time there that most people thought I lived in the projects, too. Many respectable and successful people today have their roots in McRae Homes.

There were no designer clothes back then, so we all dressed the same way. Most of the boys' daily school wardrobe was a pair of dungarees or blue jeans with a white t-shirt and sneakers. When we got holes in our jeans from playing marbles or baseball, our mothers would sew patches over the holes; no self-respecting Southerner would be caught dead wearing torn jeans with holes in them. Girls wore cute dresses or skirts with ribbons or barrettes in their hair. Each of us had Sunday clothes that we could only wear on Sundays when we went to church or to a fancy school function like graduation.

In the Bottom, there was a great co-existence among the six barber shops, four taxi services, twelve food vendors, two dry cleaners, two funeral homes, a doctor's office, a tax service, a pool hall, a police substation, and a boys' club. Some of the names were Brady's Barber Shop, Britt's Barber Shop, Clark's Barber Shop, Coleman's Barber Shop, Grimsley's Barber Shop, and Sheffield's Barber Shop. The taxi stands included John Henry's Rolling Cab Co., Farby Rambo's Taxi, Shelly Jacob's Taxi and Porter Chambers Dothan Cab Services. The soul food cafés and nightclubs were The Tea House, Shack's Grill, Turner's Café (T&T), The Oyster Box, John Henry's Café, The American Legion, The Citizen's Club, Jackie's Lounge, Jan Bouier's Lounge, The Ebony Lounge, The Blue Front, and the Club Capri.

Dr. William H. Greenfield, Dothan's only Black doctor, had his general medical practice in the Bottom; he was trusted and respected by all the people in the Bottom because he probably delivered most of them as babies. Dr. D. V. Jemison, Jr., Dothan's only Black dentist, operated out of an area called Five Points on the other side of town. The Blacks who lived near Five Points, Lakeview, and Acid Plant Hill have their own stories to tell.

Nearby Dr. Greenfield's office was the William Washington Hotel and Hawk's Funeral Home, both owned and operated by Mr. Marion Hawk. Mr. Hawk owned almost all of the commercial buildings in the Bottom; he was a very wealthy and respected Black man. He and his wife, Mrs. Alvetta Hawk, were instrumental in establishing the Hawk-Houston Boys' Club, which was a lifesaver for many young boys in the community like me. The Boys' Club, renovated from the old Rufus Davis Carver Theater, gave us a safe and supervised haven to play and learn such games as checkers, chess, billiards, ping-pong, tennis, archery, horseshoes, swimming, basketball, baseball, and football. There was also a book repository where we could check out books to read. The other funeral home was named Levite Funeral Home, which was located about a block away. People conveniently lived, worked, played, and died in the same half-mile radius back then. The churches and the graveyards were still segregated.

The Club Capri and Shelly Jacob's Citizen's Club were the two largest and most famous Black adult night spots or speakeasies. The Dothan Elks Club was also a popular Black club, but it was located on the other side of town near the Martin Homes Housing Project. On the weekends, uniformed soldiers on leave from nearby Fort Rucker Army Base could be seen partying with the pretty Bottom girls. Conversely, the pretty Bottom girls often traveled to Fort Rucker to party with the soldiers. One way for them to escape the Bottom life and see the world outside was to marry a soldier.

In addition to having two great local house bands in The Dothan Sextet and Little Lois and the Capris, the Club Capri was able to convince several famed Black entertainers to play there during what some called the "Chitlin' Circuit." The Dothan Sextet was the backing band on James and Bobby Purify's big hit, "I'm Your Puppet." In the 1960s, before there were things like MTV, most of the Black entertainers traveled by tour buses to reach their entertainment destinations. We were always delighted to see the musical tour buses roll in through the narrow streets in the Bottom.

Some of the well-known musical acts that played in the Baptist Bottom at the Citizen's Club, the Club Capri, and the Dothan Elks Club were Ike and Tina Turner, B. B. King, Bobby Bland, Millie Jackson, Al Green, Tyrone Davis, Joe Simon, Peggy Scott & Jo Jo Benson, Joe Tex, Clarence Carter, and The Five Blind Boys gospel group. Soon, Dothan was able to attract some of the bigger Black musical talent to play at the Dothan Farm Center or the Dothan Civic Center. Groups like James Brown and his famous band,

The Impressions, The Chi-Lites, The Temptations, Archie Bell & The Drells, The Dramatics, The Platters, The Staple Singers, Percy Sledge, The Drifters, The Soul Children, Betty Wright, Ted Taylor, Candi Staton, O. V. Wright, King Curtis, and many more all played in Dothan.

There was a small police substation called the West North Street Precinct manned primarily by three Black police officers: Sgt. Harding Miley, Officer Gus Huntington, and Officer Charles Williams. Officer Williams was married to Dr. Francina Williams, who later became the curator for the Dr. George Washington Carver Interpretative Museum that was renovated from an old segregated Greyhound Bus station downtown. The officers kept the peace in the Bottom and other Black neighborhoods to make sure our residents were safe at night. Reportedly, these Black officers had no jurisdiction to arrest any White citizens. They would have to call White police officers if a White person needed to be arrested and booked; frequently, some Whites could be seen at one or more of the night spots in the Bottom. Most of the police officers' time was spent trying to deal with a man called Homeless Jake. Also known as Mr. Jake Wells, he was a grown man with a child's mind; he was harmless, but most people avoided him. He sometimes slept on the streets in the Bottom, where he could be seen sprawled out on the sidewalk or a bench. He was probably the first homeless person I ever saw, and my heart wept for him because I did not understand or even realize that we were poor, too. As material things went, we had a rented house to live in, food to eat, and clothes to wear, but not much more than that.

Dothan was deemed "the Peanut Capital of the World." During the National Peanut Festival time, Mr. Hawk got permission to block off the streets in the Bottom at night and have a huge street dance with a live band; today, that would look like the Foster Fest celebration in downtown Dothan. Everybody turned out for the street dances, including the whole McRae Homes Project and First

Baptist Church members. Street dances were fun, with the food establishments selling mullet fish sandwiches, sausage sandwiches, chicken sandwiches, and pork chop sandwiches for twenty-five cents each. Corn dogs, flavored water ice, and candy apples for the children could be purchased too. The street dances were usually held on a Saturday night so that partygoers could also be churchgoers as they would leave the Bottom and go straight into church wearing the same smoke-filled and alcohol-smelling attire. It was often said that these folk could stumble from Saturday night fever to Sunday morning believer in a few steps.

The best thing about living in the Bottom was all the different characters that inhabited it. There was Mr. Charlie Griffen, who claimed to have spent only one year at Oberlin College in Ohio, one of the first colleges in the U.S. to admit Blacks in 1835. Mr. Griffen was very smart, but he was also a heavy drinker. He was often seen sitting inside Sheffield's Barber Shop, entertaining waiting customers by spouting off things that he claimed to have learned from his days in college. He acted like he had a PhD and could often be heard saying things like, "When the Constitution became constipated, the Bill of Rights became bulimic." Of course, no one knew what he meant or what he was talking about. Years later, I researched what he had said and realized he was making sense way back then, but no one had taken him seriously.

The biggest character of all was my father, Mr. James L. Thompson, Sr., better known as "Shacklebones." He served in the army in WWII and was briefly stationed in Marseilles, France. The story goes that my father used to be tall and so skinny like a skeleton that everyone called him Ol' Shacklebones. When he married my mom, she fattened him up, and everyone just started calling him Shack for short. My father might remind some of the Red Foxx character from Sanford and Son, except my dad was taller. He was a natural comedian, and everyone knew him. He was often seen with a cigar in his mouth that he chewed but never smoked. He was a

17

construction worker by day and a café owner/operator by night. Shack's Grill was famous for pigs' feet, chitterlings, hot dogs, oysters, and hamburgers, but he didn't sell fish or barbecue.

There are many hilarious Baptist Bottom stories about my father, but my favorite is the time he was taking a bath, and he spotted a bottle of thick green Prell shampoo that my mother had purchased to wash her hair. Thinking that it was mouthwash, my father reportedly used the shampoo to gargle with after taking his bath. About twenty minutes later, he was seen walking toward his Shack's Grill café when he stopped on the street and started throwing up. Everyone saw all these hundreds of bubbles coming from his mouth and didn't know what to think.

Reportedly, my father later went home and scolded my mother by telling her not to ever buy any more of that mouthwash again. My mother, not knowing what he was talking about, went to the bathroom to see half of the Prell shampoo gone. She died laughing after realizing what he had done and told everyone. Of course, my father did not think it was too funny. I still laugh when I think about how he must have looked with all those shampoo bubbles coming out of his mouth.

Right next to Shack's Grill was a place run by a man named Mr. C. R. Kelly but whom everyone called "Kiss Pig." To this day, I never knew how he got that name, but he was a very comical man, and the nature of the business he ran was called a liquor joint. Mr. Kiss Pig, as we children called him, was a very strange-looking and -acting character with a very weird name.

Homeless Jake was probably the next most famous inhabitant of the Bottom. He could often be seen walking around with an axe so he could make money by chopping down someone's trees, whether they needed chopping down or not. People would often pay him a few coins not to chop down the trees and just leave. Looking back now, I think Homeless Jake was a very smart man; he ingeniously figured out how to use the axe as a prop to get paid without doing any work at all.

There were many other characters and unforgettable people who populated the Bottom in the good old days. Some of the names and faces that I will never forget are Lorraine "Lois" Armstrong, Rusho Miley, Farby Rambo, James Sneads, Eunice Owens, R. C. "Yank-Yank" Hurt, Shelton Gifford, Patricia "Pussy Cat" Feagins, Long Tall Ressie Barnes, Professor Abner Jackson, Pensy Coleman, Doug Malone, Clinton Morris, Shelly Jacobs, Andrew Bell, John Fordham, Charlie Clark, Amos Sheffield, Ben Sheffield, Otis Grubbs, JT Clark, John "Chat" Thomas, Frank Neal, Hot Dog James, Luke Casey, Boy Kirkland, "Red" Randy Flournoy, Nana Gooten, Milton Foster, Johnny "Pig" Jackson, Ronald "Fat Jack" Jackson, Ronnie Scott, Charles "Bop" Turner, and a man called "Tip Light" because of the way he walked on the tips of his toes due to a deformity.

A few months ago, I reconnected via telephone with a childhood friend whose family had lived in the Bottom in McRae Homes; his father owned and operated one of the barber shops there back in the day. As we were reminiscing about the good old days in the Bottom, he said, "Man, we should rename the Baptist Bottom 'Wakanda Dothan' because we were so self-sufficient back then, like Wakanda in the *Black Panther* movie." First, we laughed at the idea, and then we said, "Yeah, why not?"

So, with this writing and the power vested in me, I hereby rename the Baptist Bottom WAKANDA DOTHAN. There should be a sign or marker somewhere near to deem this locale as a historic part of Dothan.

Hollywood has finally realized all the Black gold that can be made from making movies regarding the Black experience; the first *Black Panther* movie grossed over one billion dollars, and the sequel was released in 2022 and called Black Panther II: Wakanda Forever.

It may be too late or too costly to bring back the Baptist Bottom in all its glory as we knew it then, but there is a Baptist Bottom

Revitalization Plan in the air that might bring back some of the flair, independence, and pride to a neighborhood now seen as underserved. The McRae Homes Housing Project has been renovated with a facelift, but it is still there. A multitude of residents have died off, and many of the buildings in that locale have been demolished; only a few of the historic buildings remain, like the First Baptist Church (the Boys and Girls Club now) and one or two other buildings. The hotel, funeral home, all of the eating establishments, taxi services, dry cleaners, and police precinct have long disappeared. The Garden of Eden now resembles the Sahara Desert.

I recently drove past the area formerly known as the Bottom and was dismayed at the desolate sight. None of the gardens, fruits, vegetables, or pecan trees remain that used to be there. I parked my car, got out, and walked near where Shack's Grill used to be. There was nothing there except an empty lot and all of the memories left behind.

Suddenly, I heard a buzzing sound over my head, and I looked up to see a UFO in broad daylight. Then I realized what I saw was a drone being piloted by a nearby father and his young son. I walked over and asked them what they were doing. The father told me he was teaching his son about drones as part of a new school STEM program to help him get ahead and be part of the future. Our young people have to be ready to move ahead and not be left behind like my memories. I knew from my experience that STEM was an acronym for Science, Technology, Engineering, and Mathematics. I smiled and thought if Hollywood can make *Black Panther 2: Wakanda Forever*, there is hope in revitalizing the Baptist Bottom. I crossed my arms in front of my chest, bowed my head, and whispered, "WAKANDA DOTHAN FOREVER!"

# TO CARVER WITH LOVE

Like flowers, children grow best when watered with love.

In the wilds of an unsophisticated jungle, it is a very rare thing to see lions and tigers playing together, but yet they played. However, in my genteel, Southeastern Alabama hometown, it was impossible to witness the Dothan High Tigers play the Carver High Lions in football or any other sport due to the unrepentant "separate but equal" school ideology that permeated the South before integration.

In the South, separate-but-equal was *Critical.* It was about *Race.* It was about *Theory.*

Fair play was thought to be separate but equal; however, it was always known that there was no truth in that educational misnomer. For example, students from Black schools sometimes received hand-me-down schoolbooks from White schools with racial obscenities visibly scribbled on some of the pages.

Dothan's George Washington Carver High School was a segregated but self-contained public high school serving African American children from 1940 to 1968. In 1969, the students were integrated with White students at Dothan High School, and Carver High was closed forever. The high school was gone, but the history, heritage, and contributions of a great school live on through its former students, teachers, and their descendants. My sister, Anita Thompson, graduated from Carver in 1968, and she went on to become an extraordinary city planner and later a teacher before she passed away in 1987.

Artis Gilmore, the legendary 7'2" NBA basketball superstar, played for the Chicago Bulls and the San Antonio Spurs before he retired. In 1967, Gilmore graduated from Dothan's Carver High School, where he was a giant basketball sensation. Gilmore may be the most famous graduate of Carver High to date, but his skills and talents were indicative of the kinds of students that Carver High bred.

The renowned Dr. James A. Smith served as principal of Carver for the bulk of its existence. Dr. Smith was a resolute administrator and a caring and protective educator. He cared for his students and his school like a shepherd guarding his sheep. Under his leadership, he had a diverse teaching staff, and all of his were not Black. Before mandated integration, there was one Caucasian teacher, Mrs. Burnelle Armstrong, who taught English at Carver. Mrs. Armstrong was educated at Samford University. There was also one Asian teacher, Mrs. Kozue Armstrong, who also taught English and was educated at Tokyo, Japan's Aoyama Gakuin University. Mrs. Kozue Armstrong was the daughter-in-law of Mrs. Burnelle Armstrong.

Carver High left a rich legacy and history of which to be proud. The Carver High basketball team won the AA state championship for the 1957-58 season. The Carver High Marching Band, known as the "Marching 100," was widely believed to be the best high school band in the state. They were frequent performers at the Dothan National Peanut Festival, where Blacks and Whites marveled at their superb showmanship. If you ever got a chance to see the Marching 100, you were always amazed at their acrobatic athleticism and homegrown, honed musicianship.

In addition to being strong in sports and music, the students at Carver were also academically strong. Carver had the Willie Kathleen Idlett Chapter of the National Honor Society, whose credo was *Leadership, Scholarship, Character and Service.* There was the Frederick D. Patterson Chapter of Future Teachers organized in 1953, and it was an affiliate with state and national education associations. Carver had the Bi-Phy-Chem Club, which was a science club that represented biology, physics, and chemistry. There was the Future Business Leaders of America (FBLA) Club, the International Thespian Society, the Choral Program, the Art Club, the Math and Algebra Club, the Student Council, and Carver had a Vocational Trade and Industrial Educational component that focused on careers like auto mechanics, brick foundation masonry, and cosmetology. At their graduation ceremony, Principal Smith charged the class of 1969 to build their fortune according to their chosen theme: "Education – the Blueprint to Progress."

When Carver was closed and the students were forced to attend Dothan High School, the separate but equal doctrine began to break down. The band members of the excellent Marching 100 were not seen as equals to the band at Dothan High. Their music styles and marching formations were completely different and based on their respective cultures and environments. It was assumed that the Carver students could not read music and therefore were subpar. The Carver band members served as sort of a "B" team band to Dothan High's band as they had to audition for their spots in the Dothan High band. The Carver students greatly resented that assumption, and that resentment has lingered for decades. The former members of the Carver National Honor Society and other clubs felt shunned or not accepted as they had been at Carver. It was a bitter pill to swallow for seniors from Carver during that first year of integration, and that may help to explain some of the blatant disconnect among the students who do not feel the need to attend class reunions for Dothan High.

Many students from Carver felt like they received a raw deal after integration and were unable to reap any benefits from it at all. Although many of Carver's students did attend college and had successful professional careers, there were others who did not and could not. At Carver, some felt like a big fish in a small pond; yet when they got to Dothan High, they felt like a small fish in a big pond. Their world was far different than what they had previously perceived and some suffered from paranoia. Some were paralyzed by various life-changing racial phobias that were more real than imagined. And the prospect of trying to get ahead in life by serving in the military was not a good prospect for some at that time because the Vietnam War would await enlistees. Left without other career options, some students did volunteer for service, and some were drafted. Some came home. Some didn't. But the ones who came home were never the same…then and now.

The 1969 Carver High School yearbook was the only one ever produced by the school. It was named GEWACA, which was an acronym that stood for the name of the world-renowned and esteemed slave-turned-scientist, Dr. George Washington Carver of Tuskegee, Alabama. The prophetic foreword in the book reads: "The GEWACA is Carver's first yearbook. It is about you -- the good and bad moments you have shared with friends. It is hoped by the GEWACA staff that our first yearbook will serve as a nostalgic treasure of memorable events of Carver at work and play. To those of other times and places, we offer the GEWACA as a history of our past and an indication of our future. A future in which we hope to make our mark on society…and, departing, leave behind us footprints on the sands of time."

The words to the "Carver High Alma Mater," lovingly written by Carver High librarian, Mrs. Emma N. Walton, offer another haunting tribute to a school that was never able to reach its full potential due to the fate of integration and progress.

> *Dear Carver High, Mother of mine*
> *We come to you with hearts sublime,*
> *Our homage to lay at your feet,*
> *For cares you've tendered so complete,*
> *We love thy wall and campus green,*

*Where e'er we go your stars are seen,*
*Your name inspires, your colors fly,*
*Like herald banners in the sky.*

*Chorus:*
*O Carver High, Dear Carver High*
*Voices we raise from earth to sky*
*To tell thy virtues we proclaim*
*A fond recall of Carver's name.*

*Symbolic with your name is one,*
*Whose fame will last 'til day is done*
*Like His whose models were the clay,*
*May all your virtues reign for aye,*
*Benevolent, protecting true,*
*Our hearts are thine what'er we do,*
*Through ages and eternity*
*With reverent voice we'll sing of thee.*

*Help us dear Father as we pray*
*Keep our dear school from earth's decay*
*Long may her meteors blaze with light*
*To steer the path on darkest night,*
*Grant wisdom, power, and grace divine,*
*To all who seek a higher climb*
*Within these walls of ageless dreams,*
*For guidance from your radiant beams.*

As a ninth grader in 1969, I was destined and eager to attend Carver like my sister Anita; however, our schools were abruptly integrated and at the last minute, my dreams of Carver were short-circuited. Although I was never part of the historic Carver High, I did manage to be a part of another kind of history in that I was a part of the class of 1972, the first graduating class of Dothan High that had three full years of integration. For me, integration forced me to compete and become better. I carried the credo of Carver High in my heart and tried to live the words of Carver's alma mater. Many of the teachers at Lake Street Junior High School told me that I was not as smart as my sister, and that helped encourage me to do better at Dothan High School. It was true that Anita was the smartest sibling in my family, and I could not hold a candle to her academic record or scholastic achievements. At Dothan High, I forged my own path but carried myself like I was a transfer student from Carver High. I knew that I was different but I also felt that I wanted to make a difference.

The smell of fear filled my nostrils as I first walked through the halls of the human jungle at Dothan High. With the heart of a lion and the eye of a tiger, I realized that I was now a half-breed – a LIGER. This was the first time that lions and tigers interacted together on a sophisticated level. Integration had unwittingly created a new breed of hybrid students from Carver, now ready to play on a future field that would be more level than before. We slowly moved away from separate but equal toward a competitive world that focused on the survival of the fittest. Carver students had proven that they were fit and able to compete on any world stage, just like Artis Gilmore had demonstrated before.

"To Carver with Love" is an apt title for my essay because I firmly believe that, like flowers, children grow best when watered with love. Some may wonder who would have won the game between the Carver Lions and the Dothan Tigers had they been allowed to play. The answer is simple: we all would have won! I hope in some way that this essay will help heal some of the wounds of the past and help us all to understand that all of our actions in life are like footprints on the sands of time. We have to be responsible for our own well-being and ensure that we also look out for others who may be struggling. "All for one together" is the motto that we all should live by.

> "Some men see things as they are and say why. I dream things that never were and say why not."
>
> – Robert Francis Kennedy

# "MARITAL CHOREOGRAPHY"

Marriage is a dance best choreographed by two people who have pledged their lives together. Many marriages start with a two-step, then foxtrots into an elaborate but delicate waltz that serves as a lifelong mating ritual. The one who leads the dance is the one who has majority control.

I never learned how to dance before I got married. Stepping on toes was a common occurrence as I struggled to try and lead. Being led taught me how to finally gain enough confidence to lead, but it came with a high price and a painful lesson: "When learning to dance, one should start out in their bare feet without any shoes."

Marital Choreography is necessary to maintain a healthy marriage and avoid the pitfalls of divorce, especially for those unwilling to learn to dance. Gracefully popping your fingers and shaking your hips may qualify as minimal dancing or "faking it" for the uncoordinated and the dysfunctional; however, doing the Twist, the Funky Chicken, the Macarena, or the Electric Slide is more preferred. In order to be a proficient dancer, one must have skin in the game, but they must not be thin-skinned.

Obviously, some people dance better than others and are lighter on their feet. When caught in a jam or a web of lies, some resort to breakdancing and pop-locking. Others excel in doing the Robot with a little tap dancing added for guilty showmanship. One of the best dancers I ever saw was a man who did the Moonwalk for two blocks after his wife caught him cheating with another woman.

Fast dancing is the best dance to do when you need time to manufacture a good alibi. With the music blaring loud, one can pretend he didn't hear the twenty questions being asked of him. Slow dancing is for cool professionals who take everything in stride and always have their A-game in their back pocket. One should never take a slow dancer seriously.

Finally, women always dance better than their male partners because their bodies are more elastic and limber. When lying, they contort their bodies into inhuman shapes and positions to make their partners believe their lies. Instead of men buying a Life Alert system, they need to invest in a Wife Alert system to tell them when she is being untruthful.

Since my wife taught me how to dance, I consider myself as proficient a dancer as James Brown or Michael Jackson, especially when I'm trying to explain how I couldn't call home to say I would be late because I had a flat tire after hitting a deer, my cellphone was not charged, and I sat in my car for three hours waiting on AAA. Now, every time I leave home, I always bring my dancing shoes.

# NAKED TRANSPARENCY

Conventional wisdom inhibits me from disrobing my decency and shedding my desire for naked transparency. For many reasons and on many different levels, I cannot do what I really want to do or say what I really want to say. Today's etiquette protocols, social mores, and political correctness will not allow me to shock the system with the tiniest spark by erecting my manhood to its natural Homo sapiens state to become my authentic self. After all, what is manhood if it cannot be seen without the constriction of camouflaged coveralls? Make no mistake; I am talking about the desire for unabridged human expression and not pornographic nudity here.

In order to unzip the zipper to the societal facade around me, I must first be willing to understand and accept the various modern-day consequences of doing such an audacious thing. In a short story by Danish author Hans Christian Anderson, an absent-minded emperor walked around naked for days without fear or concern of any community criticism until a child yelled out, "The Emperor is naked. He has no clothes on." This expression is now often used to describe a situation in which people are afraid to criticize something or someone because the perceived wisdom of the masses is that the thing or person is good or important. This fairy tale appeared in Anderson's book *Fairy Tales Told for Children,* published in 1837. Although the famed story did not signal the birth of conformity, the emperor was made to conform by updating his attire to be more pleasing to the community. With or without clothes, he was still the emperor. Isn't that the larger point of naked transparency?

All humans have an equal set of chromosomes that total twenty-three pairs times two for a total of forty-six. The twenty-third pair, identified as the sex chromosomes, differs between males and females. In other words, half of our chromosomes come from the father and the other half from the mother. Although invisible to the human eye, these genetic designations called DNA identify us and make us who we are regardless of our personal preference or permission. We are uniquely who we are, and we must remain true to ourselves in order to fully realize our potential and accept the destiny of who we really are. If red hair, freckles, and a dark complexion are part of your genetic heritage, then be who you are without succumbing to plastic surgery or hair dye to become a clone of someone else. You deserve to have all the naked transparency that you were inherently given.

Putting icing on a cake, paint on a car, or lipstick on a pig does not change the inherent nature of any of these things. A pig is still a pig, a car is still a car, and a cake is still a cake underneath. We should love and cherish who we are underneath it all. The next time someone accuses you of not being transparent, unzip your pride and show them what you've got.

# AMERICAN ME

What makes me an American? Does just being born in the United States make me an American? Does having a U.S. birth certificate, Social Security number, driver's license, and passport automatically make me an American?

It feels like I was born with a built-in identity crisis. My birth certificate identifies me as Colored. In grade school, I was labeled a Negro. In college, I was deemed Black. Today, I am considered African American, although I have never been to Africa. I've even heard some people ask, "Why don't you go back to Africa?" In this instance, the "you" meant a collective "they," and the sense was that "we" should not get too comfortable being here so far away from home. Where is my proverbial home?

I read that in the 1920s, Marcus Garvey, a Black nationalist in America, actually started a movement called "Back to Africa." His organization, the Universal Negro Improvement Association (UNIA), represented the largest mass movement in African American history. Garvey and the UNIA established 700 branches in thirty-eight states by the early 1920s. Garvey admired Booker T. Washington and was greatly influenced by Washington's book, *Up from Slavery*. He developed many of his organization's ideas around some of the principles from Washington's book. Through the UNIA, Garvey pushed to support the "Back to Africa" movement and created the Black Star Line to act as the Black-owned passenger line that would carry patrons back and forth to Africa. He also fostered restaurants and shopping to encourage Black economic independence. Garvey's UNIA established the motto: "One God! One Aim! One Destiny!"

Both confused and encouraged by what I read, I wondered what my DNA ancestry would show. Curiosity got the best of me, and I ordered a DNA kit to see what my bloodline would reveal about my ancestry and my true heritage. Within a month or so, I received my results. Based on the saliva swabbed from my mouth, my DNA yielded the following results: African: 91.6%; European: 6.6%; Admixed American: 1.4%; South Asian: 0.5%; and East Asian: 0.2%. The 91.6% African category was further broken out into such micro details as Esan in Nigeria: 32.6%; Yoruba in Nigeria: 15.2%; Mende in Sierra Leone: 11.3%; Luhya in Kenya: 10.7%; African Caribbean: 9.6%; Gambian: 8.4%; and African American: 3.8%.

So now, combined with both imagination and science, I feel I have a more complete understanding of my person, my set of circumstances, and my birthright. Like a native seedling planted on American soil, I sprang forth here, yet my roots extend all the way to Africa and beyond. Only my ancestors have the right to urge me to go back home to bask in the sunlight of my creation. I will visit my ancestral home with great pride when I get the opportunity. In the meantime, I will remain here in America to celebrate the "me" I have become through migration, education, and assimilation. Incidentally, the color of my skin should be insignificant to my race: Human Being.

# FREEDUMB

Freedom is a widely misunderstood word. Many believe that it is a basic human right, while others proclaim that it is free. History has taught us that both of those assumptions have been proven wrong. For many in the world, freedom has not been a basic human right, and for many others, freedom definitely has not been obtained without a very high cost. Why is there such a wide disparity of thought and agreement on what freedom actually means and is?

The real answer to the question of freedom often depends on where you were born, where you live, and how much wealth your family may have. Unfortunately, in America, 10% of the people have 90% of the wealth. How much wealth you have can directly impact how much freedom you may have. It's interesting how I can sometimes walk around with a pocketful of money and never think about eating or buying anything. On other occasions when I am flat broke, I get so hungry that my stomach starts growling, and I want to buy everything in sight.

In this country, we have altered the word *patriot* to only mean military or law enforcement personnel; however, that is so inaccurate. Anybody can be a patriot regardless of their professional title. I contend that teachers, mechanics, plumbers, home builders, taxi drivers, cooks, and homemakers are all patriots – especially if they support American values. Being a patriot carries a certain freedom, just like being a native-born citizen, in most cases.

I was born in the South in the 1950s, and there were times when I questioned how free I was. Legal slavery had long been abolished, but Jim Crow laws and segregation were the laws of the land. Our public schools in my hometown were just integrated in 1969, a little over fifty years ago. Prior to that, we were not able to live as free as others were. Thankfully, some people were able to figure out that a person's race, creed, or gender should not have a bearing on the freedom of law-abiding, natural-born citizens.

It is very dumb to think that every person is not entitled to be free. George Orwell's 1945 satirical and allegorical novella, *Animal Farm*, is the perfect realistic book about how some humans think and act. In the book, the animals foolishly proclaim that "all animals are equal, but some animals are more equal than others." Unfortunately, there are still a lot of believers today in that myth. Freedumb is a contagious disease of the mind that is slowly becoming a pandemic.

# REINVENTION

Lately, I've been reading a lot about innovation, reinvention, and improving upon what we already have. Usually, this talk concerns some of the most successful products in history that may not have been invented first but were best to market, making them the most successful.

As I thought about everything I read about reinvention, I wondered if it was possible to relate the same principles to my personal life in reinventing myself. I remember reading stories about people who reinvented themselves and went on to live different, more satisfying lives. I became convinced that I could do the same thing. My favorite stories are the ones where the successfully rich corporate executives quit their jobs to start teaching public school in low-income areas to help the less fortunate reach their potential or where the longtime hairdresser of more than thirty years left her job at age forty-five to fulfill her dream of operating her own dance school, or where the Wall Street executive was laid off after twenty-five years of service and found herself out of work and useless at age sixty. The executive moved to the country and bought a farm with some alpacas; now she has one of the most successful alpaca-breeding businesses in the country. These examples of self-reinvention really inspired me.

When I retired from my twenty-three-year career as a federal criminal investigator, I needed a positive way to think about myself and my accomplishments. I wanted to become successful again and relevant in other endeavors. I felt I needed validation in my life for not only the things I had done before but to go on validating myself as a productive human being. I wanted to continually feel good about my life so that it would seem worthwhile. I was still young enough to believe I had more to contribute to society. Previously, I had found success at being a teacher, a writer, and a federal agent. Without realizing it, I had been reinventing myself every time I changed careers and started something different and new.

I had found the key to my reinvention by just living every day and changing my perspective on life. In order to go forward with the idea of reinventing myself yet again, I needed a plan to understand what I wanted next and how I expected to get there. I devised a one-step personal guide to help me find my next venture and adventure. That important step was just realizing I needed to change my attitude and prepare my mind to accept new things. Easier said than done. That one simple step made all the difference in the world to me. I started researching new careers to gauge my interests. Luckily, I quickly found that acting and filmmaking were things that piqued my interest, especially since I was already a movie buff.

Reinventing yourself is not a difficult thing to do once you make up your mind to just do it.

# THE INTERMISSION

"Stop the world, I want to get off!"

Sometimes, we need to take a break from the overload of unsolicited information, misinformation, and disinformation that daily bombards us. There are far too many continuous "talking heads" fraudulently disguised as news, politics, religion, entertainment, advertisement, telemarketing, infotainment, etc., that we cannot keep up with or make sense of. This constant noise and confusion present major distractions from what should really be important to us and make it almost impossible to set our real priorities in this life. There is no longer any such thing as a simple life. As consumers, we are far too consumed with everything from epidemic to pandemic and from feeding the needy to feeding the greedy.

In earlier days, the theaters would show movies that included an intermission. Those fifteen-minute breaks would allow the patrons to go to the bathroom or what have you, but at least they were given a short reprieve. Today, with twenty-four-hour television and radio programming and all-night movie theaters, there are few intermissions. Consumers are overloaded with too much noise and not enough peace and quiet.

Constant gunshot sounds and frequent car chases disturb the peace in many ghetto and suburban neighbors. Amber alerts, robberies, assaults, and break-ins are more common today than ever before. Good Samaritans are hard to find these days, and we barely know how to communicate with our neighbors for fear of our own lives.

Most households today receive between fifty to one hundred unsolicited spam calls per week from unavailable phone numbers. Junk mail has recently slowed some, but there is still an abundance of unwanted consumer mail in the trash cans.

American television viewers are receiving horrible lessons in civics as we constantly watch our politicians find lower depths to descend to. The original idea of government being "of the people, by the people, and for the people" has long been lost in translation in favor of the egomaniacs masquerading as our political representatives who only represent themselves.

The lesson here is that we have to create our own intermissions by tuning out, unplugging, and creating safe zones within our homes. We deserve some time to hear our own selves think; peace and quiet today is a premium quality, and we should claim some for ourselves before it's too late. PEACE!

# WAY BACK WHEN

Ever wonder what happened to the Black Power fist and the peace sign? Were they fads that faded along with Afro puffs, platform shoes, and popcorn shirts? I shall never forget the stir caused by African American Olympic runners Tommie Smith and John Carlos when they raised their black-gloved clenched fists over their heads during the playing of the U.S. national anthem at the 1968 Summer Olympic Games in Mexico City. That simple silent gesture later got them banned for life by the International Olympic Committee (IOC) and expelled from the Games. The IOC obviously viewed the gesture as rebellious and militant. Yet, in hindsight, that gesture was a very proud and historic moment for a lot of Blacks. Why? Because we viewed the extended fist as an extension of the Civil Rights Movement that was well under way by then. It gave birth to funky words like Black Power and Afrocentricity. Later in the decade, boxing heavyweight Joe Frazier began his two-year reign as champ by using his powerful Black fist to knock out Jimmy Ellis. I imagine at that time, his victory song was James Brown's "Super Bad."

In the 1970s, I remember feeling especially soulful and proud as I strutted down the street like a peacock. After I'd spent all day picking out my 'fro to perfection, I'd slide on my big apple hat, put on my red, black, and green polyester jumpsuit and my platform shoes. I felt both clean and funky. When I met another Brother or a Sister, I'd raise my arm, clench my fist and say, "Right On!" Back then, I'd always get a mirrored response from the Brother or the Sister acknowledging my presence. Those were the days when being

Black was being Black, and Blacks were not afraid to greet each other in public.

During that same time, James Brown's pulsating Black national anthem, "Soul Power," electrified the radios and the record players at all the house parties and gave us a surge of ethnic pride. All over the streets, people in my neighborhood were echoing the words to Marvin Gaye's "What's Going On?" and "What's Happening Brother?" Some of us were even "digging the scene with a gangster lean" as we cruised in our cars with "sunroof tops and diamonds in the back" while we jammed to William DeVaughn's "Be Thankful for What You Got." Of course, we didn't have much, but we were very thankful for what we had.

In those days, Blacks were not the only race "rebelling" against the conservative norm with long hair, wild clothes, and loud music. Young liberal Whites created the "flower power generation" and made freedom and fashion statements with beads, bell-bottoms and bushels of flowers. Flashing the two-finger peace sign all over the place, some Whites even sported their "permed" version of the Afro. If there was indeed a racial awareness or an awakening taking place, both Blacks and Whites were experiencing it together.

In 1970, four students were fatally shot by National Guardsmen during an antiwar demonstration in Ohio at Kent State University. The first Earth Day also debuted in 1970 and suggested that "environmental protection" would be a global issue. All the music from the now legendary Woodstock concert, along with Tommy James and the Shondells' "Crystal Blue Persuasion" and Don McLean's "American Pie," will always be associated with the time when all of us were discovering our American heritage and learning about each other in the process. The common denominator then was the confusing Vietnam War that Blacks and Whites all tried to make sense of to no avail.

And when the peace sign looked like it was on its way out, it resurfaced in another form during the Nixon administration.

President Richard M. Nixon grew famous for raising both hands and displaying two peace signs to create his famous victory symbol; he was being "hip" in order to win the election. By the time President Jimmy Carter took office, the country seemed to be striving toward change with a more diverse racial make-up. The bicentennial year (1976) brought experimental "biracial study groups" that re-examined the race situation and tried to find solutions to the age-old problems. Still a distant galaxy away from true racial harmony, the diversity in the country was beginning to look different, and it was a lot different than it had been just ten years earlier. The American Dream was no longer seen as a "once upon a time" fairy tale; some believed the long struggle was beginning to pay off for Whites and for minorities. Of course, history did not record the next twenty-five years as anything to brag about regarding the end of racism. There were still struggles and there were still "pay-offs," but that was then; this is now.

Recently, I was in a crowded "corporate America" elevator with some other prominent Brothers and Sisters. To my surprise, everyone remained tight-lipped, and no one spoke to each other or even acknowledged the presence of each other. When I did manage to catch the eye of a young Brother standing next to me, I smiled and said, "Hi!" He only looked away and pretended he didn't hear me. Later that day, I was walking downtown, and I ran into a former classmate I hadn't seen in years. I recognized her before she saw me. When we approached each other, I said, "Hello, Debbie!" She looked away and kept walking as if she didn't hear me. I said, "Wait, Debbie. It's me, James." Then she stopped, turned around and said, "Oh, James, I didn't recognize you. I thought you were just some brother trying to hit on me."

How did we get to this point? Whatever happened to people greeting each other in public with pride? The Black Power fist was a part of our cultural legacy that has slowly disappeared if not outright died from public view along with other traces of our Black culture like blues and jazz. These genres used to be popular Black music, but now we seem to have abandoned that music for something else.

Luckily, some of the importance of the teachings of historical leaders like Malcolm X resurfaced during the 1992 release of Spike Lee's movie about slain hero Malcolm Little. During this time, Blacks (and some Whites) everywhere could be seen wearing the "X" logo on caps, shirts, jackets, shoes, eyewear, etc. Unfortunately, the "X" fad has now faded, too; we'd be hard-pressed to still find the "X" logo on anything anymore. In 2014, we saw the premiere of the movie *Selma* about the life and death of Dr. Martin Luther King, Jr., another slain hero. Notwithstanding these two films, historic films about us and our contributions are few and far between.

The late Marvin Gaye's "Inner City Blues" (1971) and the late Prince's "Sign of the Times" (1986) provide musical similarities and food for thought to the notion that history repeats itself. Both beloved musicians were "Right On" when they sang about the degradation of our society and ourselves as we fight losing wars against drugs, Black-on-Black crime, and the re-establishment of the Black family. Marvin Gaye's "What's Going On" and "Mercy, Mercy Me" are still as relevant today as they were when released over fifty years ago. We seem to be regressing instead of progressing.

I recently learned that the Afro hairstyle and bell-bottomed jeans are making a fashion comeback. At first, I asked, "Why?" And then I realized it's just a fad, a phase of life that will come and go as fast as blaxploitation films and platform shoes. What goes on our heads should be replaced with what goes in our heads. Likewise, instead of new shoes, we need a new direction for our feet to take us if we only learn from the things that happened way back when.

# BUFFALO SOLDIERS:
# FORGOTTEN HEROES REMEMBERED

April 22, 1994, will always be a day to remember in Dallas, Texas, and around the world. On this day, some "forgotten heroes" were proudly remembered 128 years after an 1866 Act of Congress (July 28, 1866) authorized the formation of six African American regiments in the peacetime Army prior to the Civil War. These six all-Black military units encompassed two cavalry (9th and 10th) regiments and four infantry (38th, 39th, 40th, and 41st) regiments. The Black infantrymen were subsequently merged, renumbered, and renamed as the 24th and 25th Infantries. These soldiers were respectfully nicknamed "Buffalo Soldiers" by the Native Americans mainly because the Black soldier's "wooly" hair reminded them of the sacred buffalo known for its raw strength and fierce courage.

The U.S. Postal Service enshrined the Buffalo Soldiers in memory with the issuance of a twenty-nine-cent commemorative stamp. But the Buffalo Soldiers commemorative stamp is not just another stamp with a Black face. The stamp, designed by Mort Kunstler of Oyster Bay, New York, was officially dedicated in Dallas by Marvin Runyon, the Postmaster General and CEO of the U.S. Postal Service. Paying his respects by wearing a Western hat and a bolo tie, Runyon unveiled a twelve-foot-high replica of the stamp commemorating the Black cavalry units that helped settle the West. The stamp colorfully depicts a lesson in history that is virtually invisible in history books.

The honored guests of the ceremony held at the Hyatt Regency Dallas at Reunion were keynote speaker U.S. Navy Commander Carlton Philpot, who is also Chairman of the Buffalo Soldiers Committee, and former Buffalo Soldier, Sergeant Mark Matthews, Sr., U.S. Army Retired, 10th Calvary, 1917-1947. They both paid tribute by wearing the hats and scarves of their early counterparts. Sergeant Matthews was visibly moved when the stamp was unveiled and when Philpot vowed to continue the efforts to have the Buffalo Soldiers commemorated at the Smithsonian Institute and in history books by the year 2000. After being presented with a special Buffalo Soldiers plaque by Runyon, Sergeant Matthews gave his stamp of approval by striking a pose in a soldier's "salute" to the audience.

Over several decades, Buffalo Soldiers served in forts throughout the U.S., including Texas, Arizona, New York, California, Louisiana, Oklahoma, Montana, Utah, Nebraska, Virginia, Vermont, and Kansas. Fort Scott, Fort Larned, and Fort Leavenworth in Kansas were a few of the strategically important posts protected by Buffalo Soldier regiments. In fact, Fort Larned was the key to the protection of the Santa Fe Trail.

The attitude of the U.S. Army toward the Black soldiers during the Civil War and the Spanish-American War may account for the reason the Buffalo Soldiers story is considered a "missing page" in American history. It is said that the Buffalo Soldiers endured cruel hardships and routinely received inferior food, equipment, and horses. However, the Buffalo Soldiers received the highest number (eighteen) of Congressional Medals of Honor and had the lowest desertion rate of any Army regiment from 1867 to 1898. In addition to engaging in fights with Native Americans, they confronted outlaws, desperados, protected stage and railway lines, strung telegraph wires, guarded frontiersmen against bandits and cattle rustlers, and "rescued" Teddy Roosevelt and his Rough Riders during the Spanish-American War.

In his book *The Negro's Civil War*, James M. McPherson documented that "although over 178,985 Black men enlisted in the

Union Army during the Civil War and fought in 449 engagements, of which thirty-nine were major battles, and in spite of the fact that approximately 37,300 Black soldiers died wearing Union uniforms, their military accomplishments were never fully appreciated, especially by the military leaders." And William H. Leckie wrote in his book, *The Buffalo Soldiers*, that "there were many white officers who looked upon an assignment with Black soldiers as undesirable. So strong was the prejudice against Black soldiers that some white officers preferred to take a lower rank in a white regiment as an alternative to duty with a Black regiment. George Armstrong Custer, when offered the rank of lieutenant, turned it down, hoping to get an appointment in a white regiment."

Although history has not been mindful of the accomplishments and contributions of many unsung African American heroes like the famous Tuskegee Airmen, the Negro Baseball League, or the Buffalo Soldiers, at least now the U.S. Postal Service is trying to right some of the wrongs. Ironically, the Buffalo Soldiers, who were expected to lick the boots of other regiments, are literally being licked by Americans everywhere every time they mail a letter.

Note: From 1941 to 1946, the famed Tuskegee Airmen were known as Buffalo Soldiers in the sky as history repeated itself.

# THE NEED FOR VALIDATION

Miracles happen daily. I once read about a New York City beggar who won over $50 million in the lottery. When asked how she was going to handle her newfound wealth, she smartly replied, "First, I'm going to get a job and become a respectable citizen."

"A job?" asked the dumbfounded reporter. "But why? You're rich now. You don't need a job."

"But being rich is not like having a trade," she said. "I want to have a real job so I can feel like I belong to something. I can't write homeless person or millionaire in the box reserved for occupation on my tax form."

Preposterous, you say? Well, not really. The need for human *validation* is a real thing. Although somewhat unexplainable, humans do possess an irrepressible need to belong to someone or something. It is a nondescript feeling but one so strong and important that a streetwise beggar-turned-millionaire felt that she needed an occupational title in order to be valid. In spite of her wealth, she still has the common need to belong.

"Will you please *validate* my parking ticket?" said the middle-aged man to the hotel clerk. "Of course, Mr. Smith," said the clerk as she stamped his ticket. Mr. Smith tipped his hat, said "thank you" to the clerk, and ran off with a modest smile. Perhaps Mr. Smith or the desk clerk hadn't realized it, but more than the parking ticket had been *validated* during that short exchange. Each received a generous acknowledgment of their existence pertaining to their respective positions. The attention and respect that we receive from others help to give our lives meaning.

From an infant holding tightly to his daddy's thumb to a suckling calf clinging to her mother's breast, all creatures seem to have the need for *validation*. The infant is an infant and the calf is a calf, both separately and logically identifiable by their differences and their likenesses. In a ferocious world of identity crises and distorted values, there is no substitution for the feeling of self-worth. To have *validity* in our lives is to have truth and to feel successfully alive. No matter if you're a bartender, a professor, a plumber, or a beggar, you should feel secure enough to be true to your station until change affects it.

None of us were created to be beggars or millionaires, but we were all cut out to be workers in the melody of life who should be able to pursue every endeavor without fear of failing and becoming losers. After all, success and failure depend on the perception we have of ourselves at the time. If you feel you're a success, you are; if you feel you're a failure, you may fail unless you change your perception.

From preschoolers to college grads to grandparents, we are constantly tasked to decide what we are to become to help give our lives more meaning. Being compatible with and accepted by our peers is an important incentive behind the exhaustive search for validity, yet even before we've been accepted by our peers, we still need to be accepted by those three little inner peers -- the *Me, Myself and I* of the soul.

Years ago, my grandmother had the urge to go back to school to get her high school diploma, or GED. Amused by the idea, my father discouraged her from pursuing that goal by pointing out she was too old to go back to school. My sisters and I thought it was pretty funny, too; we all giggled when we imagined Granny sitting in a classroom wearing an apron. Granny smiled and never brought up the subject again. A year later, Granny died without obtaining her diploma. I had forgotten about that until I was recently watching a Senior

Citizens Tournament on the TV show *Jeopardy*. The "old" people featured on that episode were in their eighties and nineties but were incredibly smart. Uncontrollably, a tear fell from my eyes for Granny. I knew then that she had felt unfilled and *invalid* at not getting her diploma. And to think, we made fun of her when she attempted to pursue it. Since then, I swore never to make fun of anyone's pursuit of happiness again, no matter how odd it seems to me. Live and let live so we all can feel *valid* is my new philosophy of life.

By trade and career choices, I was a law enforcement officer, a teacher, a salesman, a youth counselor, a construction worker, a dish washer, etc. In each job, I felt a strong sense of self-worth, although my true longing is to someday be a writer. I don't exactly know why, other than it's what I feel I need in order to be *valid*. Money does not seem to play a major role in this urge I have. Throughout the years, I've written many papers, poems, articles, essays, short stories, etc., but I still wonder if I have what it takes to become a successful writer. "Success"...there's that word again. Like the beggar, Mr. Smith, and Granny, I long to have *validation*.

"Thanks for *validating* my ticket," said the young man as he handed his ticket to the parking attendant and sped out of the garage into the roaring traffic of the city where miracles happen daily.

# Short Stories

## (1,000 WORDS OR LESS)

*"Imagination is the beginning of creation.*
*You imagine what you desire, you will what you*
*imagine, and at last you create what you will."*
– George Bernard Shaw (1856-1950)

# HOW TO GET AHEAD AT WORK

Yawning, I gazed out the window at the beautiful Halloween afternoon. I saw a flock of birds heading south, and I heard the wind chimes lightly clanging from the cool breeze blowing over my porch. The phone then rang to mock the chimes and interrupt my serenity. Although it was my day off, I knew the life of a crime reporter was governed by the increased crime rate purported for our city. I rushed out the door without my backpack but had to go back and get it; I'd forget my head if it wasn't attached to my body.

I sped to the location the news desk had given me, hoping the assignment wouldn't last all day. It was a wooded area out in the country near a rifle range. I saw a state trooper walking by and asked him where the crime scene was. He pointed to a spot ahead where a few other officers were headed. The trooper said, "Watch yourself, it's a pretty gruesome scene. I had to step away, but I'll head back in a little bit." I thanked him and kept walking until I reached the scene. I first saw the boots on a body that was covered with a white sheet; the top of the sheet was bloody wet with an alcoholic stench.

"Gonna be kinda hard to identify this guy without a head. He's been decapitated," said Cloyd Perkins, the medical examiner, as he briefly pulled back the sheet to let me take a peek. I flinched as I reached for my iPad to document the scene.

After a few minutes, Cloyd said, "Hey Roy, will you stay here with the body while we jet over to the IHOP to grab a bite? We'll only be gone for a few."

"What? You mean you want me to stay here with the body, alone...by myself?"

"Yeah, the corpse is dead, and it ain't gonna bite you."

"But...."

Before I could finish my sentence, Cloyd waved his hands with, "We'll only be gone for a few," and he left with the rest of the troopers. There I stood with my backpack and iPad looking down at a bloody, headless corpse covered with a white sheet. I glared around, and all I could see was wide-open country with plenty of huge cornfields and tall trees. The sky darkened as the stubborn crows cawed and flew overhead like vultures that suspected I was a human scarecrow preventing them from feasting.

I was getting ready to take some pictures with my camera when out of the corner of my eye I saw one of the feet on the corpse move. "What the hell!" I said as I jumped back away from the body and started to run. Its other foot moved and started to shake. Then the hands on the corpse reached out and slowly pulled the sheet down from where its head used to be. Not waiting to see what happened next, I ran as fast as I could, leaving my backpack behind.

My plan was to drive quickly to the IHOP to alert Cloyd and the troopers to what I had witnessed. When I got to my car, I saw Cloyd and the rest standing there laughing their asses off.

"What's going on, guys?"

Cloyd was holding a small radio-controlled remote control. He said the corpse was a robotic dummy he was operating from a distance, and they had videoed the whole thing. He then said, "Trick or Treat...it's Halloween, man!"

"You mean this whole thing is a prank, and there is no crime scene?"

"No, man, we were just pulling your chain on your day off. It was all for fun."

"Guys, you scared the hell out of me. I hate decapitated bodies!"

Just then, Cloyd's radio went off, and we all heard the police dispatcher say,

"Cloyd, we have a Code 3 over on Country Road 666. Get your team ready because this is a gruesome scene. The locals are over there trying to identity a decapitated man. It looks like the body's been out there since early this morning. What a damn shame, you know…it being Halloween and all."

Cloyd looked at me and said, "Roy, sounds like you got your headline for this one already written: *How to Get a Head at Work for Halloween!*"

Everyone laughed but me. In disgust, I decided to head, uh *leave,* for the crime scene.

# LOCKER GIRL

Her locker was next to mine at school. Hers was on top and mine was on the bottom. She never spoke to me, and I didn't know her name at first, but she unwittingly inspired me to set my locker's combination to L36-R24-L36 so that I would never forget it. Even if I didn't know her name, I wanted to get as close to her as possible. I dreamed of the day that she would legitimately notice me.

Once, we met at our lockers at the same time. It was an awkward encounter for me. I just stood there staring and waiting for her to enter her locker first. She quickly opened her locker, pulled out a book, and walked away without even looking in my direction. Embarrassed, I observed that she didn't use a combination to open her locker, so I decided to leave her an anonymous note from a secret admirer. Just when I was about to put the note in her locker, she suddenly came back and caught me with her locker door wide open. I sheepishly said, "I must have bumped your locker door by mistake as I was trying to get to mine." She smiled and said, "It's okay." Then she held out her hand and stared at me. I popped up from my locker and looked at her quietly. She abruptly said, "Why not just give me the note you were trying to leave in my locker?" I said, "Note…what note?" She said, "The one still in your hand." Like a deer caught in headlights, I lowered my head to look at my hand and slowly passed her the note. She stood there, read it in front of me, smiled, and said, "Thank you" and walked away. I felt like such a fool and couldn't wait until the end of the school day so I could drag myself home. It was painfully obvious that she had no interest in me and was only toying with me and my affections. In my head, I could hear her telling her friends about our encounter as they all laughed hysterically.

The next school day, I hurried to my locker so I wouldn't have to run into her again. I had planned to change my combination as soon as I could devise a new one; I even considered asking the school office for a new locker on another level. I quickly opened my locker and reached in to get my notebook. My eyes spotted a pink sealed envelope that I did not recognize. I picked it up and brought it closer to my eyes. It smelled of perfume and had a note inside that read, "Hi, Locker Boy. In a rush yesterday you forgot to lock your locker. I must have bumped it open by mistake, but I wanted you to know that your secret is safe with me. I think you are sweet and handsome, and I would like to get to know you better." Signed, Locker Girl.

# THE SPELLING BEE

The Wilson High School Spelling Bee was scheduled, and my teacher, Mrs. Curtain, enrolled me because I was a good speller. Although I was only a sophomore, I would be given words suitable for more experienced students, and I would be spelling against some of the best. Betty Gere had won the competition three years in a row, and she would be hard to beat. Because of that fact, I trained daily with Mrs. Curtain and felt I was ready for the challenge. I was confident that I knew all the big hard-to-spell words, and I even read the dictionary just for fun.

On the day of the contest, the competition was fierce, and we battled for forty-five minutes straight; I was selected as one of the three finalists, along with Betty Gere and Dolby Sims III. As it was a three-way competition now, Dolby was up first at bat. Principal Bloodstone, the moderator, looked at his long list of words and asked Dolby to spell the word *defunct*. Dolby smiled really wide and proud because he knew he had it in the bag with an easy word like that. Without even thinking about it for a second or giving the moderator a chance to finish his sentence, Dolby looked out at the crowd and yelled out, "Defunked, D-E-F-U-N-K-E-D!"

The crowd went silent. Principal Bloodstone frowned and said, "No, that's wrong. The correct spelling is D-E-F-U-N-C-T." The crowd then loudly booed Dolby. He was so crushed he ran off the stage crying; he knew his parents were expecting him to win. Now it was down to Betty and me. She pranced up to the microphone next and waited for the moderator to give her a word. She was short with freckles and red hair and Betty was super smart. In fact, most people called her Super Betty. The principal looked down at her and asked her to spell the word *Teutonic*. Betty paused, looked up into the air, and then said, "Teutonic, capital T-E-U-T-O-N-I-C." Principal Bloodstone smiled and shouted, "You are correct!" Betty said "thank you," shot me a smirk, and took her seat.

I slowly walked up to the mike as nervous as I could be; I had lost my cool after seeing Dolby turn into a crybaby. The principal asked me if I was ready. I grimaced and said, "Yes, sir." He carefully searched his list and then looked up and asked me to spell the word *orgasm*. I hesitated and tried to envision the word in a sentence. After about fifteen seconds, I blurted out, "Orgasm, O-R-G-A-N-I-S-I-M." Instead of going silent, the crowd burst into laughter. I didn't know why everyone was laughing because I felt I had nailed it. Principal Bloodstone just looked at me in disgust and shook his head before announcing Super Betty as the winner and four-time champion. With the crowd still buzzing, Super Betty walked over to me and whispered, "You idiot, even I know what an orgasm is and apparently you don't."

Obviously, I was crushed. When I got home, my parents and my brother were waiting to see if I had won. I told them that I did not win but I came in second. My parents were not impressed and demanded to know which word I got wrong. I told them the word was orgasm and that I thought I had spelled it right with O-R-G-A-N-I-S-M. My parents looked at each strangely, and my mom told my dad that he needed to talk to me. My dad deferred to my brother and told him to talk to me, and then they left the room in a hurry. My brother put his arms around me and took me to his room. We sat on his bed for a minute, and then he said, "Boy, you got a lot to learn. It's a good thing you got me as your big brother. An orgasm is something that can create an organism if there is a consensual agreement between two people. You understand?" I shook my head "no" because I didn't know what he meant.

My brother then put on some music by Barry White and told me to listen to him to get a better idea, and then he left me alone. After about an hour of listening to Barry White, I felt a little *defunked*, but I still didn't know what an *orgasm* was.

# HOLLY'S CURIOUS CUISINE

On the campus of Luverne University in southeast Mississippi, Willie met Holly in the school cafeteria approximately two years after the assassination of Dr. Martin Luther King, Jr. The school's student body was newly integrated, but the institution was not yet tolerant of liberal ideas or new students who strayed beyond their place out of the norm due to an unnatural curiosity. Sitting quietly and awkwardly among their classmates and teachers eating lunch, Holly asked Willie to please pass her the pepper. Without looking at her, Willie slid the shaker over but kept his head down.

"That's the salt shaker; I need the pepper," Holly said.

Surprised, Willie looked up from his plate at the cute freckled-faced strawberry blonde and said, "Sorry" and slid the pepper over to her.

"Thank you," Holly politely said, then smiled.

"You're welcome." Willie did not smile for fear that his gesture might be taken out of context. Because of the times, he was conditioned to remain stoic. Holly then looked at him and asked his name. The teacher sitting closer to Holly overheard the exchange and looked at them with disapproving eyes. Willie looked down and away and softly answered, "Willie. Willie Banks."

"I'm Holly Adams," she said, extending her hand for a shake.

Before Willie could extend his hand, Mrs. Troy, the teacher, asked him to pass her the salt and the pepper. Maybe it was the way she put a special emphasis on the words "salt and pepper," but it caused Willie to focus on them and realize how different they were, like him and Holly.

When he did pass them to the teacher, she said, "Thank you, Willie!" with a glint in her eye that he interpreted as a subtle warning. He remembered fourteen-year-old Emmett Till, who was killed in Mississippi for his "unnatural" curiosity. Holly dropped her hand when she realized Willie was not going to shake her hand in public.

Throughout the school year, Willie and Holly uncomfortably avoided each other, especially being alone anywhere together. Since they were in the same department, they took most of their classes together, but their friendship was interrupted by fear, and it was never allowed to take root. The faculty at this peculiar institution was pleased they remained in their respective places. Holly was inducted into the honor society and got busy doing the things her major demanded; Willie, who majored in Journalism, was promoted to the editor of the school paper. After four years, they both graduated on time and went their separate ways without the orientation they desired.

Twenty years later, Holly was relaxing at her Houston home and reading the Sunday paper when she came across an article titled "Why Black History Month is Important." The byline of the article was William S. Banks of *The Dallas Morning Times*. Holly immediately thought of her classmate Willie Banks from her college days and said that it couldn't be him. To be certain, she sent an email inquiry to the address listed after his article. The next day she received a reply from William Banks that simply said, "Hi Holly, you found me. You got the right Willie Banks from Luverne University." Holly screamed because she was ecstatic to hear from Willie again and reconnect. She told her sister and intimate friends all about Willie or as much as she knew, and they also seemed excited to meet him. Holly said over the years she thought about Willie and wondered where he was, and it turned out he was just four hours away in Dallas.

Over the next months, they caught up by sharing conversations, photos, stories, and writings via email. Holly teased Willie about not shaking her hand that day; Willie responded by saying he was sorry and should have. He promised to visit her in person soon and take her to lunch somewhere other than a college cafeteria. Holly, now a gourmet chef, counteroffered to prepare lunch for him at her Houston restaurant, Holly's Curious Cuisine.

When they finally saw each other in person, Holly and Willie enjoyed reconnecting and promised to remain friends forever. Each of them had matured into beautiful and handsome people. They discovered that what seemed to have been short-circuited from the start was actually a premonition of a lasting friendship to come between two people who had more in common than not. During lunch at Holly's restaurant, she smiled brightly, her red hair shining and no more freckles. She coyly asked Willie to pass her the pepper. Willie smiled and passed her the salt on purpose.

"You remembered," said Holly.

"I did," said Willie.

# PASSING THE BAR

When Ben Richards passed the bar, as difficult as it may have been, he felt a great sense of accomplishment. He called his friends to tell them the news, and they naturally threw a festive party in his honor. They all knew that Ben's passing the bar was a step in the right direction, but they also knew that it was just the first step in his ten-step plan. You see, Ben was an alcoholic, and his passing the bar without stopping for a drink meant that he was trying to beat his addiction and go cold turkey. Step 1 was to empower yourself, not your addiction. Things would get easier if he stuck to the plan.

Julie Jansen, Ben's girlfriend, organized the party and wanted Ben to know that his friends supported his efforts toward sobriety every step of the way. Besides, Julie wanted to marry Ben one day and have children; she did not want her kids to emulate Ben's drinking habits, though. John Gimbel, Todd Stuart, and Chuck Widener, Ben's best friends, lifted him up and did a victory dance with him on their shoulders. Even Ben's pastor, Reverend Mathis, stopped by to wish him well. When the party was over, Julie told Ben that she loved him and would always be there for him.

As time went on, Ben moved to Steps 2-3 of his sobriety plan, which involved recognizing your weaknesses and remembering the bad times. Ben knew he was weak for alcohol and no longer wanted to wallow in the guilt of all those times he woke up drunk with a bad hangover. He wanted to marry Julie too, but not in his present condition, so his motivation was to kick the habit altogether. Steps 4-6 included knowing why to quit, outer talk, and inner talk. Ben had his reasons for quitting, and he was now listening to his outer voice ("I don't drink alcohol because I want to look and be healthy") *and* his inner voice ("I know that what I am doing is right"). For Steps 7-8, Ben was asked to have a dirty mind and see the healthy you. The dirty mind was to picture the evil images of alcohol consumption and the damages it could do; the opposite of those images was to see in his mind the healthy, new person he was becoming. He was well on his way to changing his and others' perception of who he was.

Steps 9-10, the final steps, involved day-to-day actions and the company you keep. Ben had a good grip on following through with his actions from the outlined steps, but more importantly, he realized that he needed his friends to keep him grounded. Julie, John, Todd, Chuck, and all the rest were critical in making the circle complete toward Ben's final success. By now, he was beginning to say to himself that "sobriety feels good," and he owed much of his success to the good company of friends in his circle.

Ben knew that passing the bar was an ambiguous phrase and joked that in the past he was never able to pass the bar without stopping in for a few drinks; now "passing the bar" took on a whole new meaning, because it was about raising the bar to a higher level of health and happiness.

# THE WARMEST DAY OF OCTOBER

I t was a cold October morning as we all stood outside together, holding hands and warming each other with the blood that ran through our collective veins. An air of peaceful respect ruled the day. There was not a single incidence of violence or disrespect shown to any person present. I remember the reverence and quietness with which we stood, as if linked together by an invisible chain made of guilt, shame, love, peace, atonement, and forgiveness. A soft humming of an old Negro spiritual could be heard as we held fast to each other and looked toward the makeshift stage that resembled a slave auction block near the Washington Monument.

The exact date was October 16, 1995, and I was one of the many who attended the Million Man March in Washington, DC. One of my best friends told me that he and his father were attending together, and they invited me to go along with them. I was living in Philadelphia then, and I hadn't originally planned to attend the march; I had not considered the wider significance or the impact of men of color from all stations in life coming together in mass to atone for the sins perpetrated against each other. Collectively, we were also atoning for all the sins against all the women of the world that have been disrespected, misled, or betrayed, including our own sisters, wives, girlfriends, and mothers.

The Reverend Jesse Jackson was one of the guest speakers on the dais that day along with numerous other luminaries. He shouted a stirring speech that resonated with the crowd and reminded us of the fire that Dr. Martin Luther King, Jr. had lit about thirty-two years earlier with the same cadence in the same location. Reverend

Jackson's voice resounded, "I am somebody! You are somebody! We are somebody! Together we can make a difference. Today is the first day of our reconciliation with ourselves and the sins that we have allowed ourselves to collectively commit. After today, we will not return to the way we were because we will have atoned for our sins both to God and to our fellow men, women, and children. We are a million strong today. It's the way nature planned it. Together we stand. Divided we fall. God bless us all. Amen."

It was a short speech, but its words contained enough power to influence our thinking and illuminate our feelings. We cried, we hugged, we asked each other for forgiveness, and we promised to be changed from that moment on. My friend and his father were swallowed up in the moment like I was as we passed along expressions of love to other men who had been strangers to us before that day. At the end of a long historic day filled with good wishes and pride, we bid our newfound brothers warm goodbyes and returned to our car for a quiet ride home. We didn't speak because our hearts were still full, and our minds were trying to process all that had happened that day. I wondered if the feelings of brotherhood within me would last and if I would really be changed after that day. I told all of my friends about my experience and that I was one of the men at the Million Man March. I told them that it wasn't really a march but more like a wonderfully huge revival meeting. I said, "We were a million strong that day, and it was the way nature planned it."

The thought of men coming together to publicly proclaim atonement for sins committed against women and each other weighed heavy on my mind over the next few days. I really wanted to make a change and a difference in my life and the lives of others. As I sat in a near-deserted theater the following Monday waiting for the feature presentation to begin, I noticed a young man and woman hurriedly pass me by and disappear up in the top seats where others weren't; it was odd because they didn't have any popcorn and they seemed eager to get to their destination. A few minutes later, I heard a giggle, and I looked up only to glimpse the man because the girl was out of sight. I reasoned what they must have been doing, and I realized this was an example of what our recent atonement was about – our corruption of women and our self-respect.

When the young man took a break and went to the lobby area, I followed him. He went into the men's room, and I did also. Once we were in the light, I could tell that he was a teenager. As he was washing his hands, I said hello to him and told him that I remember being his age and bringing my girl to the movies. He looked over at me, smiled, and said, "Cool!"

I added, "But I always respected her, and I never did anything with her that I might regret later on. She was my girl, and I loved her. I hope you feel the same way about your girlfriend."

He stopped washing his hands and sheepishly looked over at me. I smiled and softly said, "I am somebody. You are somebody. We are somebody." And then I walked out the door, hoping he would get my meaning.

As the days of October went on, I found myself spreading the word about atonement more and more to all of my friends. I honestly felt and truly believed that the Million Man March made me see life differently and want the best for all of us. I also knew that my personal atonement started with me, and I must practice what I preach. From that point on, I set out to right many of the wrongs I had committed in my life. I called my estranged father to tell him that I loved him and wanted us to be closer. Over the phone, I heard my father cry for the very first time.

# THE DNA SEEDS

Across the street from the shopping mall near the interstate, in plain view, sat the blue BMW used as the getaway vehicle in the recent robbery of the New Centurion Bank. I'd never heard of this bank before, but this was a big city with a lot of banks; every other day, it seemed a bank was being robbed by some thugs who wanted to get something for nothing. In the thirteen years I had been on the force, I had never liked working bank robberies. Something always went wrong, and I could tell that this one was no different because something just didn't feel right. Maybe it was the way the car was parked on the curb or maybe it was just where it was parked that got me to thinking more than usual.

The license plate TZA-1562 matched the one called out over the radio to all law enforcement, and there could not have been two identical BMWs with the same plates. I simultaneously pulled my gun and called the dispatcher to report that I had sight of the vehicle and was approaching it for a closer look. The dispatcher acknowledged and sent out additional units to my location. The windows of the getaway car were darkly tinted, so I couldn't tell if it was occupied or not. The closer I got to it, the more nervous I became, thinking I might have to fire my weapon for the second time in my career. The setup looked as if the bad guys may have conveniently selected the spot next to the busy interstate for a quick and easy escape. The car was most likely stolen and wiped clean of fingerprints or any evidence that would allow us to catch the criminals fast, but as a matter of department protocol, we had to call in the Crime Scene Forensics Unit.

In a matter of minutes, two unmarked police cars with lights and sirens sped onto the scene to serve as backup until the regular patrol cars showed up. I recognized both of the undercover officers, Jim Cooper and Frank Neal, as they blocked the entrances with their cars to let me know they had my back in case someone was hiding inside the car. Both officers got out of their vehicles and aimed their guns at the BMW. I tried to peek inside the window of the driver's side, but the windows were too dark. I hoped the car was not booby-trapped with explosives or any type of biochemical weapon. Before doing anything else, I decided to wait and let the forensics guys make the call on entering the vehicle to get more information on the crime scene. Then I heard a muffled sound coming from the BMW's trunk. I hurriedly signaled to Frank and Jim that there might be somebody in the trunk. Both of them walked slowly toward me and the suspect car, their sights locked onto the trunk as if they Expected an Army to pop out. Both men were former members of the department's SWAT team, and they were expert marksmen. At that point, five marked patrol cars screeched in, with officers jumping out and taking cover behind their cars. Capt. Samson yelled, "What've we got, boys?" as he walked toward us with a pump-action shotgun. I told him I heard a noise inside the trunk, and we were waiting for them to come before we made another move.

Capt. Samson ordered one of the officers to pick the lock on the trunk. When the trunk was opened, everyone was stunned at what we found. We saw an Asian male who was hogtied with masking tape and wearing a white lab coat. After removing the tape from his mouth, Capt. Samson asked him his name. The man identified himself as Dr. Chen Wu, director of the New Centurion Bank. Dr. Wu said he operated a sperm bank and two men robbed him at gunpoint and took hundreds of live specimens with them in a silver footlocker. The doctor said he overheard the men say they were going to sell them on the black market to countries that were looking to grow their own people from scratch and train them to kill Americans. In disbelief, Capt. Samson immediately called the office to have them call in the FBI and alert the White House. This was the beginning of the international case known as the DNA Seeds.

# MISSING:
# THINGS LIKE THIS
# DON'T HAPPEN

Heidi, Demecia, and Amber were best friends on a shopping spree at Providence Hills Mall. This year, their parents had given them money to independently shop for their school clothes at the upscale mall. They were dropped off by Amber's mom, who had given them three hours to complete their selections. The girls had strict orders to stay together, not separate from each other at any time, and no fraternizing with boys. Providence Hills is one of the most secure malls in the state, with security cameras and security officers in uniforms and plain clothes.

After they spent an hour at The Gap, the girls decided to stop at the food court for a snack. They ordered their food, secured a table, and got comfortable, chatting about the other items they had planned to purchase. Leaving her purse and purchases, Heidi asked the girls to watch her food while she went to the restroom. When ten minutes had passed and Heidi had not returned, Demecia went into the bathroom to look for her. In a minute, she came running out to tell Amber that she did not find Heidi in the bathroom. Amber suggested they not panic and surmised that Heidi probably sneaked back to The Gap to buy that blouse she wanted. They went back to the store to look for her, but she hadn't been there either. The two friends hurriedly walked through the mall together looking for Heidi but had no luck; then they frantically decided to report her missing to the mall police.

The police checked all the surveillance cameras for the areas the girls said they had been, but there was no sign of Heidi anywhere. Remembering the strict instructions they had been given by their parents to stay together and not separate, Amber and Demecia began to cry as they now feared the worst. Rick Sanchez, the officer on duty, contacted the girl's parents and filed a missing preliminary person's report to the mall manager for Heidi Renee Erickson, age 15.

Two weeks later, there were still signs and posters displaying Heidi's picture and rewards for information leading to her whereabouts. Law enforcement officials added her name to the international database containing thousands of other young people gone missing in a similar way. There were no witnesses or evidence that showed the girls had run away of their own volition; it was assumed they were kidnapped for trafficking purposes. The state task force on human trafficking was not any closer to finding any of the girls on the list than they were Heidi. It was almost as if the girls had been whisked away by aliens. Kidnappings among teenage girls were now becoming common, like school shootings. Girls such as Heidi were in high demand as sex slaves and child laborers in some cultures willing to pay top dollar for these taboo services. Candle-burning vigils for their safe return were never-ending.

On November 24, 2014, a large fishing boat headed for Bangkok, Thailand, was raided by authorities, who found hundreds of chained people, including teenage males and females, being smuggled against their will. The men, women, and children were from various backgrounds and different countries; twenty-five were from the U.S., and one of them was named Heidi Renee Erickson. When the law enforcement officials monitoring the national database received confirmation that Heidi and the others were alive and well, they contacted their parents to tell them the news.

After a full debriefing and physical examination, Heidi was finally returned to her hometown on November 27. Amber and Demecia were among the crowd who cheered for her when she arrived at the airport. Upon seeing her parents and friends, Heidi burst into tears and ran to them. Heidi said a man in a mall security guard uniform kidnapped her and forced her into a van; she reported that she was okay and hadn't been harmed. Heidi said had the authorities not intervened, she would have gone to Bangkok to be sold into slavery against her will. She said she kept thinking the whole thing was a dream and that things like this didn't happen in America. When she saw all the other young people who looked like her aboard the ship, she knew that human trafficking was real. Heidi felt that she was fortunate because most stories don't end the way hers did. She now aspired to have a job that would help put an end to human trafficking.

Currently in the U.S., over 600,000 people per year go missing. The majority of them are never found. In Canada, over 80,000 per year go missing. Unfortunately, things like this happen every day somewhere in the world.

# DRUGS AND THUGS

I dreamed I auditioned for a play in NYC and won a minor role in *Drugs and Thugs*, an off-Broadway production starring Denzel Washington. I was booked to play a pompous 1970s drug-dealing pimp named Acid. It was a comedy, of course, with names like that. My character only appeared in a couple of scenes and had just a few lines, but I was determined to make the most of it. The costume department outfitted me in the stereotypical pastel-colored pimp suit with a wide-brim hat and lots of flashy, cheap gold-plated jewelry. I had to speak with a tough NY accent, although I am originally from Alabama; you can imagine what that sounded like. I also didn't know anything about drugs since I had never experimented with them before, but I am an actor, so I acted.

On the first day of rehearsal, I met Denzel Washington, and we seemed to hit it off well. In one of the scenes, I had to try and sell him some drugs on the street corner as he passed me by. My line was, "Hey bro, wanna buy some blow?" After I delivered my line, I was supposed to do a little chicken strut like George Jefferson. I looked stupid and felt silly, but that's show business, and it was the beginning of my big break. Denzel couldn't stop laughing every time I said my line because my hat kept falling off when I hit my stride. After about fifteen takes, the director yelled, "Time out!" and sent me to wardrobe to change my hat.

We rehearsed for one week, and then we were ready to open our show on September 5 for a two-week run. The ticket sales were very brisk because many of the women wanted to see Denzel. When I told my friends I was in a play with Denzel, they would not believe me.

It wasn't until I showed them a snapshot of me with him that they took me seriously.

On opening night, about an hour before the curtain call, I peeked out to see if anyone was coming; all I saw was an empty theater. The theater manager assured us that people were coming even though it was a rainy Thursday night. The manager was right because about thirty minutes later, the auditorium started to fill; you could hear the foot traffic of the people hustling to their seats. I peeked out again and smiled when I saw that all of the seats in the small place were occupied. There was a man seated in the front row who bore a remarkable resemblance to the Rev. Al Sharpton; however, I didn't really think it was him.

A soft gong sounded to indicate it was now showtime. The opening music started playing, the curtains came up, and Denzel walked out on stage to deliver a very funny soliloquy about the inherent dangers of living in NYC with all the drugs and thugs. Then the lights came on, the action started, and the street suddenly filled with furry pimps and their scantily-clad hookers dancing in the street and getting down to a funky 1970s beat. It was a typical big New York production. The pushers sang, "Wanna buy a dime bag for a nickel?" The bad girls chimed in with, "Hey baby, I got what you want and what you need. Beep-beep!" Everything was frantic and frenetic, like a circus with street clowns.

The audience laughed in all the right places and howled at all the right times. Things seemed to have been going off without a hitch until the second half of the show. The guy in the front row who looked like Rev. Sharpton turned out to be him for real. Rev. Sharpton started complaining about all the buffoonery that the Black cast members were doing, and he started a riot by calling for a boycott. Some of the audience members joined him by standing up and loudly chanting, "No drugs! No thugs! No drugs! No thugs!"

The theater manager came out and got involved by calling security and asked them to remove Rev. Sharpton and all the chanters.

Backstage, all the actors were getting worried because we didn't know what was going on outside. When Denzel peeped through the curtains to see what was happening, someone threw a shoe and hit him in the head. A female fan saw what happened and she cried, "Oh my God, they killed Denzel!" Then a whole row of female fans started cursing and looking for the person who threw the shoe. Denzel wasn't really dead, but he did get a nasty bruise on his forehead.

Then all hell broke loose when the police showed up and started arresting people until no one was left to enjoy our show. The producer and theater manager were peeved that our opening night was ruined. It was unbelievable. The night had started out fine, and I was about to get my big break when the riot broke out; my first scene with Denzel was the next scene in the play. I sat on a stool with my head down, crying, until Denzel walked over, put his hand on my shoulder and said, "Don't worry, son, sometimes that's the way it goes. There'll be other shows, and we'll get to work together again." He gave me a high five and exited the theater through a side door.

I never saw Denzel again in person, and my big break never came. I did learn a few valuable lessons, though: Learn your lines. Always be prepared. Stay away from drugs. And never eat fried chicken, collard greens, and ice cream before you go to bed at night.

# NICKNAMES AND BASKETBALL

Assembling a group of my favorite friends was an easy task for me when I was growing up. Somehow, I just seemed to gravitate to the ones who had the weirdest nicknames but who were also faithful pals. In the South, everybody had a nickname, and the names were usually awarded instead of chosen by the person. A southern nickname is a thing of pride and is often considered desirable, symbolizing a form of acceptance, but it can sometimes be a form of friendly ridicule. For instance, my nickname was Shack, which was derived from my dad's nickname, which was Shackle-bones. My best friend's nickname was Knick-Knack, and his dad was called Yank-Yank. You get the point.

One summer, I entered my friends and me in a basketball tournament at the local Boys Club. We were not NBA material, but we felt just as good as the other teams, and we wanted to win the championship trophy just as bad as anyone else. We dubbed ourselves The Bouncing Miracles, and when we played, we played to win. Skeeter and Chicken Neck were our two guards. Moon Eyes and Peanut served as forwards, and Slow Kidd and I alternated as centers since we were the tallest in the group. Our games were more like pickup games than official play, so we often played with as few or as many guys as we could find.

Our team made it to the finals, and we were up against a team called The Rimshots. They had a pretty good group with players like Sweet Willie, Bo-Gator, Slu-Lew, Hucker Buck, Sporty Red, and Snakeman. During the tip-off, I slapped the ball over to Skeeter, who immediately scored our first two points with a fancy fadeaway.

Sporty Red of The Rimshots dribbled his way past Moon Eyes and Peanut and made a three-pointer. When we got the ball, Chicken Neck danced and dodged long enough to pass the ball to Slow Kidd, who stuffed the ball in the rim in slow motion. When The Rimshots missed their next shot, I grabbed the rebound and threw it out to Moon Eyes; he scored a three-pointer from half-court and made the crowd go wild. We were now up by four. Both teams kept trading shots and making the game fairly close. At the buzzer right before halftime, Sweet Willie made an incredible left-handed shot, got fouled, and sank the extra points to tie the score.

During the second half, we scored with back-to-back points from Peanut and Chicken Neck. I fouled out of the game, and Slow Kidd became our only hope to win at center. The Rimshots used Hucker Buck and Snakeman to power their way through our defense to score at will. We were now down by six points. After a quick time-out, I told our team to feed the ball to Slow Kidd and let him slam dunk a few shots to intimidate our opponents. When he got the ball, Slow Kidd took his time going to the hoop and got the ball swatted out of his hands by Bo-Gator, who came out of nowhere to hit the fatal shot. We lost the game, owned up to our mistakes, shook the winners' hands, and walked away without a trophy. As we went home, we vowed to practice until we were good enough to win. And the next year, that's just what we did; we won the championship trophy and beat our competitors by thirty points. Funny, but some people still refer to us as The Bouncing Miracles.

# CARROT CAKE IS FOR LOVERS

The TV announcer said, "After almost a year, there is still one elusive lottery ticket holder who has yet to claim their portion of the $80,000,000 Mega Millions jackpot and the deadline to claim it is just one week from today."

"Damn," said Sheba, "Why can't I have the winning numbers? My cheap boyfriend wouldn't even loan me a five for a ticket. If I ever do win, he's not getting a penny from me."

"Come on, why be like that, Sheba? You know Jerry is a good man, and money isn't everything," said Edye. "Besides, it's the little things in life that count, right?"

"Well, Jerry got that part right…little money, little attention span, little…well, I won't go there, but you know what I mean." They both laughed but stopped abruptly when Victor walked in.

"What're you two laughing about now?"

"Nothing, babe. Sheba was just talking about what she would buy if she won the lottery."

"What about you, what would you buy if we won the lottery?"

Edye smiled and in her sexiest voice said, "I got you, babe. What else do I need?"

Then she kissed him. They had lived together for over ten years and were now considered married by common law in Texas, but they didn't seem to mind. Edye was happy to be with Victor, although they had little money; she didn't want to pressure him into marriage like Sheba was doing to Jerry. Jerry was a mechanic at Pep Boys, and Victor was in pool sales; both Edye and Sheba were hair stylists at Prime Cuts.

"Why don't the four of us go out for dinner tonight? It's on me," Victor said.

"Okay, babe, but can we afford it? I mean…"

"I got this, babe!"

Poindexter's, Victor's favorite eating place, was packed as usual, but they were seated in twenty minutes. Everything on the menu was good, and the prices were moderate. Sheba ordered salmon with vegetables and a salad, Jerry ordered a rotisserie chicken with broccoli, Victor ordered a well-done turkey burger with fries, and Edye ordered pasta with chicken and mixed vegetables. Edye specified to the waiter that she preferred no carrots since she was allergic to them. The waiter complied and took the orders to the kitchen.

"I didn't know about the carrots thing," said Sheba. "How long have you been allergic to carrots?

"All my life – I break out in hives if I eat anything with carrots in it."

The orders came out shortly, and they all began to enjoy their meals. Sheba used her fork to eat from Jerry's plate, which always annoyed him. Jerry started to complain about Edye's little annoyances.

Victor interrupted, "Hey guys, the real reason I wanted us to have dinner together tonight is that I…well, I have something to say."

Edye looked serious and wondered if Victor had lost his job or something worse.

The waiter appeared, asked if they were finished with their meals and were ready for dessert. Before anyone could answer, Victor said, "Yes, we would like to have our dessert now." He winked at the waiter, signaling him to bring out the special surprise.

"Since this is a special occasion, I took the liberty of ordering us a cake."

"Man, you're killing me. What's this special occasion?" Jerry said.

"Yeah, what's the big deal?" Sheba added.

"The big deal is...." Victor said, as he turned to Edye and got down on one knee.

"Edye, will you marry me and be my wife?"

Edye shrieked, Sheba gasped, and Jerry said, "Damn man, what are you doing?"

Before Edye could answer, the waiter presented a delicious-looking cake and placed it on the table before them. "What kind of cake is that?" Edye asked.

"It's a Karat cake," Victor said.

"But I'm allergic to...."

"I know, honey, but it's not that kind of carrot cake."

They all watched as Victor stuck his hand inside the cake and pulled out a little black box, then gave it to Edye. Inside was a fifteen-karat diamond ring!

"Honey, can you guess who the elusive lottery ticket holders are?"

"YES...I do...I mean, I will marry you! It really is the little things in life that are important and make you happy," Edye said as she gazed at her ring. Sheba looked at Jerry and slapped his face.

# ARE LITTLE THINGS REALLY BIG THINGS?

I'm not sure I completely understand the meaning of the phrase *it's the little things in life that make us happy*. I mean, the world we live in does not seem to support that claim or acknowledge us for doing little things. When I lived in Texas, it was all about the exaggerated *bigness* of things and having things larger than normal. The happy hour drinks were served in huge glasses and mugs and the steaks were usually twenty-four inches or larger in some restaurants. And it was the same when I lived in the Big Apple – things were bigger than normal there, and everyone seemed to enjoy having more, even if it did cost more. But did it make us happier?

So, what are these little things they're talking about, and where does one find them? I used to think that small things like saying please and thank you, opening doors for females, and not littering were important little things to make us happy. Now when I look around, it seems that none of those are still important. I mean, who says please and thank you anymore? Who opens doors for women, and who cares about littering? Maybe a few people still do, but generally, no one seems to care.

Telling little white lies is not considered a major sin, although a lie is a lie, no matter how small. In legal realms, they are deemed as sins of omission or half-truths rather than all-out lies. I once heard a politician tell a bald-faced lie and later, he proclaimed he just misspoke; he was forgiven for making such a human mistake. Most small crimes committed today are mitigated and reduced to fines. It seems crime does pay when it comes to little things. Are we happy yet?

I have done some little things that made me happy and were important to me. I wrote a poem a day for a month that resulted in my writing a book. I once looked up at the stars in the sky and realized that my position in the universe was like a grain of sand. Although I felt important, I knew I was no more or no less important than anything else in the world. And then I knew that big and small are based on our own limited perception; small things can be big, and big things can be small. The book *Don't Sweat the Small Stuff* was a great example of how humans worry over the tiniest of things and let them overtake their lives. Worrying about a thing doesn't make it go away or cease to exist.

There are two other common phrases that may also speak to the importance of little things that I like. One is *you can't see the forest for the trees* and the other is *stop and smell the roses*. We all know that trees, regardless of how small or large they are, literally make up the forest. And the numerous roses with thousands of scent-filled petals are each individually important when we stop and take the time to admire them. Smelling roses makes me happy. Maybe these phrases are analogous to the small things we take for granted in life that really amount to big things when all is said and done. If saying your prayers before you eat, honoring your parents, kissing your spouse before you go to bed, tucking your kids in at night, loving your best friend, watering your plants, and petting your cat or dog are all considered to be small things, then I believe little things can be big things and can make you happy.

The biggest little thing that happened to me lately was when I received an email inquiry from a long-lost friend wishing on a star to connect with me after almost forty years. Whatever little thing I did back then to make her want to connect with me, I'll never know, but it felt good to know that she remembered me and wanted to stay in touch. For what it's worth, I hope that this little essay thing makes her happy and proves to be the biggest little experience she's ever had in her life. One good essay deserves another, no matter how big or small.

# Poetry

*"Reality leaves a lot to the imagination."*
– John Lennon (1940-1980)

# IMAGINATION

All writing comes from the imagination of our mind
So that we can illustrate to others what we imagine;
we writers procreate with words.
I was blessed to have very vivid daydreams,
but even more vivid nightmares.
Are we dreaming when we are awake or
are we awake when we are dreaming?
Who knows for sure?
Creative writing is like capturing fireflies in a bottle or
a jar and unleashing them later for publication.

# LOVE SKETCHES

I drew a picture of my dream girl lying on a bed of roses
And then I drew her on a pedestal in several different poses.
Art imitating life is what I'm trying to pursue.
That is the best way for my dream to finally come true.
My artistry lightly strokes my canvas with a brush
Bringing forth a palette of colors that is so lush.
My vision is surrounded by lush and flair.
There has never been a girl like her anywhere.
What else is there for a man to draw
Than the most beautiful girl he never saw?
I won't stop until it is finally clear
That I want my dream girl standing here.
Everyone will see that I'm on a roll
When my love and I take our stroll
Off the canvas and down by the sea
Where my love and I were meant to be.
Life imitating art is the final act,
The picture of love is complete and intact.

# CANVAS LADY

On canvas,
I painted the most beautiful girl that never lived.
With every orgasmic stroke of seminal paint,
I made her come
Alive before my eyes.
I always dreamed of having a girl like her.
The more I painted, the more she came
Alive!
Naked, she fell from the canvas and became real.
I painted on some jeans and a sexy silk blouse to go with her bare feet.
We walked away hand-in-hand on our way to the beach.
A needle in a haystack is hard to find; soulmates are even harder.
She had a beautiful face, but an even more beautiful soul.
I will forever cherish this pot of gold.

# PLEA BARGAIN

Sitting down looking up at the blue-gray sky
Wondering if you're ever going to forgive me—
God knows I can't think of a good reason why
But hoping one day we can agree to disagree.
The rusty old swing set sways in the wind
As the weeds snake their way around its feet—
A year's gone by since you were my friend
I long for the days when things were sweet;
Whatever tore us apart I hope can be repaired
I miss your smile, your laugh and your disposition—
Give me another chance for my love to be declared
And make a lasting change in our current condition.
A beggar's plea is based on art instead of science
My heart is the thermostat for my emotions—
I'm betting we can make a beautiful alliance
One rooted in love, faith, and everlasting devotion;
Mistakes are bound to be made in any affair
Forgiveness is the key to a brand-new start—
Please accept my plea if you dare
And I'll love you forever with all my heart.

# WHO KNEW THEN?

Walked through the park where we first met
Our names still etched in our favorite tree;
That was long ago before my regret
Who knew then who we would be?

You grew into a famous beauty
And I became a famous writer;
Together we were very snooty
But our future was never brighter.

We got married and built a castle
Not far from where we once played;
Our lives became a hassle
And our storybook love began to fade.

Who knew then how we would end?
And live our lives separately;
The park is gone and with it went
Our favorite tree and our revelry.

# REMEMBERING EDEN

From six degrees of separation
To two degrees of admiration,
Our untrained hearts
Strayed into a Garden of Eden.
With hearts untrained to lie and
Hide what they felt, we discovered
The naked truth about what lies beneath the taboo.
In the darkness, we tasted the nectar
Of the fruit we bore and were mesmerized
By the words, perfume and proximity;
Nothing else mattered and time stood still for a second.
With one body and two hearts we felt the rapture
Of the moment and realized the urgency and the power
Within our grasp — A final kiss, a lasting embrace and
A lifetime love gave birth to a special bond.
That night young hearts ran free as wiser minds
Pledged to retain the love and respect without
Compromising what was born out of freedom.
May we never forget the night we were joined as One.

# LOVE ON MARS

My love feels like I'm beyond the stars
Reaching to higher heights with every kiss—
Any higher and I'll be loving on Mars
And this old Earth I'll never miss.
My body feels like I'm in a dream
And I'm floating weightlessly—
The gaze in my eyes is like a beam
And I'm headed toward my destiny.
Nothing on Earth ever made me swoon
My breath was never taken away—
I am somewhere beyond the moon
And believe me I want to stay.
If love on Mars is my secret place
I plan to live there forevermore—
I hope they never find a single trace
Of me, my love, and our secret door.
I'm saying goodbye to you my friend
And never coming back to Earth—
This feeling is real and not pretend
I have experienced a brand-new birth.

# PAGES OF TIME

Boxes of letters read over again until the pages turn yellow
Their words outlive us, yet the emotions remain stellar.
Ancient letters with the scent of love captured brand new
Reveal why memories don't leave like people do.
When the world gets dark and time slips away
Our letters recall when it was a brighter day.
Words born in another time but into time forever
Tell of our love together and are still very clever.
We wrote each other daily without fail
Our letters were like our kiss-and-tell;
Our mission was to fill our days with passion
Unfortunately, writing letters is out of fashion.
Now our love is in suspended animation
But it still deserves a standing ovation;
Because with love we paid the cost
Our pages of time will never be lost.

# SONGWRITER'S MUSE

A songwriter is always searching for a muse
A source of inspiration that can be used;
Trying to find the right lyric is never easy
Unless you are a prodigy named Little Stevie.
Writing from your soul is the real goal
Words come alive as your story unfolds.
A song may start out as a single phrase
And turn into something that will truly amaze.
Sometimes songs come in the middle of the night
Nothing quite like it when the feeling is right.
Writing songs is a labor of love
No better feeling that you can think of.
I've been writing songs for a very long time
Yearning for the right hook and the perfect rhyme.
When searching for the right word that you want to use
Always remember to listen to your muse.
A completed song is a gift from above
A final reward for your labor of love.

# NOT GONNA

Not gonna let my heart turn blue
Not gonna run and try to hide
To regret the love I lost from you
Or to repress the things I feel inside.
Love is a gamble – that much I know
A game that we all like to play
Sometimes a love stays, sometimes they go
But you always live to love another day.
A perfect love exists only in a perfect world
With streets of gold and milk and honey.
I have never found the perfect girl
Or won a jackpot full of money.
But again, I plan to throw the dice
And fall in love another time.
Next time I want to be sweet and nice
In order to make her totally mine.
Not gonna ever say never again
Not gonna turn my heart to stone.
For the next time I plan to win
And leave all this gambling alone.

# GOD INSIDE ME

Ever since I was young, I've felt a specialness in my soul
This feeling flowed through me like a quiet fire out of control;
Someone watched over me and held me in high esteem
I felt highly favored and a valued member of His team;
As I got older, I felt my heart stray away
And lose the closeness that I used to feel every day;
But at night in my dreams, I heard His voice
Reminding me that I was still His favorite choice.
I didn't feel I really deserved His mercy and grace
But He said that I would always have a place;
It was God's eyes on me and God inside me
That led to His kingdom and my natural destiny.
I could no longer escape what He had in store
So, I accepted my fate and longed to be more;
I now know that divine intervention is not a myth
In His image I was made to always be with.
Upon acceptance of His parental love and holy touch
I gained abundance in my life and never needed much;
There's no end to this experience that I am telling
For in my Father's house, I will forever be dwelling.

# IN REVERENCE

In memory of a well-lived life
Whose soul is now free from strife;
May God have mercy on his soul
And let him walk the streets of gold.
Nearer to God now is he
What a wonderful place to be;
Precious Lord, please take his hand
Allow his memory to always stand.
We pray that his soul will rest in peace
And our undying love will never cease;
He now walks among God's chosen few
And lives in a place that is divinely new.
We sing this song for his homegoing
With God's speed there is no slowing;
Ashes to ashes and dust to dust
In God we pray and in God we trust.

# THERE IS NO FINISH LINE

Before a race is run, we usually mark off our course and set the time,
But in life we learn there are no such parameters and no such endline.

Finish lines enable false starts and pipe dreams of coming in first;
However, the race is about having the stamina to run past the thirst.

Stopping at a specific distance is the normal measure of a race well run,
But in life stopping does not signify the end of the race because it is
never done.

When we sit on our laurels and showcase our trophies,
we don't act like winners.
In life, the real trophies go to those who
always see themselves as beginners.

We should condition ourselves to run past any preset endline set for us.
We should know that coming in dead last should be viewed as a plus.

Knowing that the last shall be first is the understanding of a virtue.
The virtue of coming in last is the symbol of our victory statue.

There is no finish line because life is a cycle without a real finish.
Even after our lives on Earth are through, our spirits do not diminish.

So, get rid of any notion that a finish line signifies you are through.
Keep on running to the best of your ability until life begins anew.

# A SHACK

Your wooden body has plenty of shattered panes and
cracked walls, but you still remain;
Your fragile frame is not as strong but you still stand;
Sometimes you feel empty and unwanted but you are still home;
And although things get cloudy and rain may appear,
the Sun still comes out and shines over your roof.
Likewise my Son – for through all the shattered pains in your heart
and water in your eyes, you can still SEE.
Through all the loss of strength in your body
and weariness in your feet, you can still WALK.
And through all the cracks in your life and holes
In your soul, you can still PRAY.

Shack, remember what the Bible says: "He forgives all my sins.
He heals me. He ransoms me from hell. He surrounds me with
lovingkindness and tender mercies. He fills my life with good things!
My youth is renewed like the eagle's! He gives justice to all who are
treated unfairly." Your life may resemble a Shack, but you still belong
to Him.

# SHACKOLOGY

What is Shackology, you may ask?
It's the study of Shack –
A nickname given to me
By friends from way back.

I was named after my dad
Who was like a rolling stone.
In the beginning I was glad
'Til I learned it meant Shacklebones.

Shacklebones meant my dad was very slim
And couldn't gain any weight;
I'm skinny too just like him
So, to have his name is my fate.

Shackology is also a style
I use to describe my prose;
It flows like the African Nile
And shines like a beautiful rose.

So, it's okay to call me Shack,
A name I now embrace;
You'll never see a lack
Of cool or pride on my face.

# EPITAPHS

From Strange Fruit hanging from poplar trees
To Black men dying on their "I Can't Breathe" knees,
Black men are still considered an endangered species
While crying out for their Mommas.

Life for them ain't been no crystal stair or diamond ring,
Ahmaud Arbery, George Floyd, Tyre Nichols and Rodney King
Modern day Black men beaten on camera
While heard crying out for their Mommas.

For the Emmett Tills, our tears are full
but our emotional cupboards are bare;
Because we know
there is no justice for them anywhere;

We currently live in a futuristic past where horrific events
are on par with current events in this 21st century.
Black lives matter… White lives matter… Blue lives matter…
All lives matter… is just idle chatter;
Because at the end of our non-stop trajectory,
no lives really matter.

# READING BETWEEN
# THE LINES OF LOVE (1970)

LOVER, I'VE HEARD THAT A
(I'm only saying
PICTURE PAINTS A THOUSAND WORDS
or painting this letter
WELL, THAT MAY BE TRUE IN
in a realistic form of words
SOME CASES, BUT THIS PICTURE
to simply tell you that
PAINTS ONLY THREE WORDS
I Love You!
IT'S KIND OF HARD FOR ME
It's not too difficult
TO SAY WHAT'S REALLY ON
to tell you this
MY MIND, SO I'M HOPING THAT
because I'm hiding my feelings
YOU CAN READ BETWEEN THE LINES.
between the lines of love.
THIS MAY BE A SILLY WAY TO
Now that I've told you once
TELL YOU THAT I CARE ABOUT YOU,
I'm going to tell you again --
BUT YOU'VE GOT TO ADMIT – IT'S A SMART WAY
I Love You.)
BECAUSE YOU'RE MY VALENTINE EVERY DAY.

# Long Short Stories

## (1,000 WORDS OR MORE)

*"Laughter is timeless, imagination has no age,*
*and dreams are forever."*
– Walt Disney (1901-1966)

# THE TEASER

Sitting in the front row in one of my high school classes, I had some pretty wicked thoughts about my ninth-grade English teacher, Miss Amanda Maze. Although she was an older woman, she appeared to be younger. She was in her thirties, but to me, she looked hotter than any teenage girl on the school's cheerleading squad. She had a better figure than an hourglass, except that Miss Maze's figure was flesh and blood. I could tell by staring at her blouse that she was hiding something inside. Underneath her thin, wire-framed glasses, she had dark, piercing eyes. Her salt-n-pepper hair was short, layered on both sides and shaggy in the back, slightly caressing her neck. Miss Maze was about 5' 6" with a small waist that accented her long, silky legs. She often wore sheer black stockings that made her legs look fantastic. She often spoke with a lisp that made her words sound sexy, kind of like a foreign language. Sometimes it was hard to understand her, but I loved the way she moved her lips when she spoke to me. I even liked the way she signed her name, using the initial "A" for Amanda to spell "A. Maze." Man, was she ever A-mazing, too! Sometimes after school, I'd ride by her house on my bicycle just to get one last look at her for the day. And believe me, all the boys in my class wanted to know where Miss Maze lived.

Even though I made an "F" the first semester, I didn't blame Miss Maze. If only I could quit daydreaming in her class. Every time she came near me, I could not stop my imagination from running wild. Although she never said anything, she had to know how I felt about her. Last week she leaned over to tell me I had a split verb in one of my run-on sentences. Gazing at her cleavage, I could only imagine what she could be hiding. She was wearing my favorite outfit, a white silk blouse with a tight black skirt that stopped just above her knees. My best friend, Bo, and I would sometimes drop chalk on the floor just to see her bend over to pick it up. Whenever she was dressed like that, I was afraid to go up to the blackboard for fear the whole class would notice my dangling participle. Unfortunately, Miss Maze had just called my name to go up to the board when the most "amazing" thing happened.

"Rrrring."

"Clath, before you're dithmithed, I want to athign your homework. Tonight, read pageth twenty-five to fifty in your book and be prepared to discuth them tomorrow. Clath dithmithed. That ith, everyone except you, Tommy. I need to thee you after clath for a moment."

"Yes, ma'am."

"Tommy, you're not doing very well in my clath. I'd like to know why?"    "I don't know, Miss Maze."

"Well, do you think you need a tutor? I could arrange one for you."

"Uh, no ma'am. My folks can't afford it."

"Well, maybe I can help you. You think you can come by my house around five thirty thith evening for a remedial lesson? My addreth ith 169 Freeland Drive."

"Yes, ma'am. About five thirty, you say?"

"Yeth, about five thirty. And remember to bring your book with you."

"Yes, ma'am."

It was only three o'clock, but I rushed home to take a shower, change clothes and prepare for my remedial lessons with Miss Maze. I wanted to at least smell fresh. I decided not to tell my folks about my remedial lessons. I'd tell them I was going over to Bo's house to play basketball or something. After my shower, I put on my Chicago

Bulls sweatshirt, starched Levis and white high-top Nikes. With my books under my arm, I rang the doorbell to her house at five thirty sharp.

"Who ith it?"

"It's Tommy, Miss Maze. I'm here for my lessons," I shouted from the doorstep.

"Oh, come on in, Tommy, ith open."

I opened the door to find her house dimly lit with scented candles. Slowly, I walked in but I couldn't see anyone in the first room. However, I could hear soft music coming from another room.

"Miss Maze..." I said, squinting my eyes to see.

"Just have a theat on the couch. I'll be right out, Tommy."

A second later, Miss Maze appeared, wearing a real short, sexy nightgown with high heels. My eyes quickly adjusted to the light. For the first time, I noticed she was wearing a gold bracelet on her left ankle. She was not wearing her glasses either. Her hair looked playfully teased, and she smiled when I stared at her. I was completely caught off-guard. I didn't know what to say or whether to look, but I stared at her anyway with my mouth wide open.

"I hope you don't mind, Tommy. I was getting ready to take a bath before we begin. To freshen up a little. Want to join me?"

"Whaaat? I mean, ma'am?"

"I thaid do you want to join me for a bubble bath before we thtart? Oh, I see you're a Bulls fan. Good, I like a man who knows how to take a bull by the horns. Ith basketball the only contact game you know how to play?" she asked, slowly turning and twisting from the room.

Not waiting to be hit over the head with a hammer, I threw my books on the floor and kicked off my Nikes without untying them first. I ripped off my sweatshirt and quickly unbuttoned my jeans. My underwear felt starched even after I took off my jeans. Then I looked down and noticed I was holding the Washington Monument below my waist. Once I was naked, I felt my way to the bathroom in the dark and slid into a huge Jacuzzi tub to join Miss Maze, who was already covered with bubbles. Man, I couldn't wait.

"Tommy, I've been watching you watching me in clath and I've been dying for a chance to tell you I think you're so thweet and handsome. You're the best-looking boy in clath and you don't have to worry about your grade. Tonight, we're going to use a rather different grading curve, if you know what I mean."

Then with a devilish grin on her face, she grabbed one of my fingers and began licking it like a popsicle.

"Uh, yes, ma'am."

"Oh, please call me Mandy."

She then slithered next to me, tickling the inside of my left thigh under the water with her fingers. I leaned back in the tub and closed my eyes, trying to appear cool, collected, and confident. Mandy came closer, kissing my chest and teasing me with her lips. I quickly lost control. I couldn't concentrate on anything but Mandy. The steam from the bath made the water bead up on me. Mandy continued kissing me with small pecks from my chest to my Adam's apple.

"Umm, Maxwell House coffee ith not the only thing that's good to the last drop. You taste good, too," she said, licking some of the water off me.

"Uh, huh," I said, keeping my eyes shut tight like Ray Charles.

Suddenly, I felt Mandy swerve around me in the tub and start nibbling at the base of my neck. Then she stuck her tongue in my ear. Grabbing my hair, she moved my head down toward the water until I said, "No, no, I can't swim."

She said, "Okay, I've got a better idea. You can wash my back. Here, let me turn around tho you can thrub me."

"Uh, huh, I mean, okay."

After I splashed some water on her, I waited for her to get up and out of the water first. That way I could finally see her full body. My face was covered with water, mostly perspiration from being overheated. She smiled, started to get up out of the water and said, "Oh, I forgot to pull the plug." Sitting very close to me, she reached under the water to find the rope for the plug to let the water out.

"There, I've got it," she said and gently tugged.

"Uh, Miss Maze, that's not the rope."

"Oh."

Standing over me, her body dripping wet, she said, "Come, it's time for me to let you rrring my bell..."

"Rrrring."

"Clath, before you're dithmithed I want to athign your homework. Tonight, read pageth twenty-five to fifty in your book and be prepared to discuth them tomorrow. Clath dismissed. That ith, everyone except you, Tommy. I need to thee you after clath for a moment."

"Yes, ma'am."

"Tommy, I called on you twice today and you didn't answer. Were you daydreaming or what?"

"Uh, Miss Maze. I didn't hear you due to my, uh, earache."

"Do you need to thee the nurse?"

"No, ma'am, it's much better now. I'll be all right."

"Well, your grade in English ith not all right. I think you'd better come by today for extra work."

"Yes, ma'am. What time you want me to come by?" I asked, smiling.

"Since thith ith your final clath, we can thtart now."

"Now? But...."

"But what?"

"Do it here? Don't you want me to come by later on this evening?"

"Don't be thilly, Tommy. We can both thacrifice a little time now. After all, you are failing my clath, you know."

"Yes, ma'am."

"If you're worried about your clathmates, everyone's almost gone. Go up to the board and I'll give you a thentence to diagram."

"Yes, ma'am."

"Oh, wait. Let me get a Coke before we thtart," she said and walked over to her desk to look for some change. I loved the way she walked. When she bent over to look in her drawer, I noticed she bumped her chair, causing a run in her stockings.

"Oh, darn. I don't have any change," Miss Maze said and walked toward me in slow motion, holding a dollar bill in her hand. The closer she got, the more I smelled her sweet perfume. Looking at her with my mouth open, I lost my train of thought.

"Tommy, do you have change for a dollar?"

"Uh, ma'am. All I have is two nipples and a dime. Uh, I mean two nickels and a dime," I said, shaking my head.

She must have realized what I said because she stopped dead in her tracks and walked back the other way, leaving me with a great view of her awesome rear wiggle. I wondered how she'd react if I told her what a big crush I had on her. Surely, she must know by now.

I walked up to the blackboard, picked up a piece of chalk, and waited for Miss Maze to come back to give me my sentence. I was praying she would sentence me to life. I threw the chalk into the air, catching it over and over again while I thought about how lucky I was to be alone with her.

When Miss Maze returned with a can of Cherry Coke, she walked over to her desk to study her textbook. I noticed there was something a little different about her. Then I realized she had removed her glasses and taken off her snagged stockings – her legs were now bare. Her hair was neatly combed, appearing neater than before. She must have stopped by the ladies' room to freshen up a little before she came back to "thentence" me. I just stared at her, mumbling to myself, "Man, this crush is getting out of hand."

"Did you thay anything, Tommy?" Miss Maze asked and quickly looked over at me with a smile.

"Huh? Uh, I said do you want me to crush your can?"

"Crush my can?"

"Uh, your Cherry Coke can...when you're through...for recycling?

"No, Tommy, I don't need you to crush my can, but thank you for asking."

"Yes, ma'am."

"Okay, let's thee how you diagram thith thentence," she said and read a sentence from her book. "In the fairy tale, Jack kissed Jill."

Dazed, I stood there for a moment, thinking about how odd the sentence sounded to me. When I wrote the sentence on the board, it came out kind of backward. I wrote, "Jack kissed Jill in the fairy tail." After I had written it, I realized I had misspelled the word "tale," changing the whole meaning of the sentence.

"Ith there anything wrong, Tommy?"

"Uh, no, ma'am. I, uh, was just thinking how I could diagram better if I had another sentence," I said, quickly erasing the sentence before Miss Maze could comment.

"Okay, leth try, 'Mary carried cookies with nuts to her guests.'"

I hesitated for a second, then diagramed the sentence. "How's that?" I said and stepped back to let Miss Maze see.

"Tommy, that thentence reads, 'Mary carried cookies to her guests with nuts.' Your modifier ith mithplaced. It looks like Mary's guests have nuts instead of cookies."

"Oh."

"I'll tell you what, Tommy. We're not getting anywhere with thith," she said, sighing when she set down her can. "Why don't you come by my home thith evening and we can finith thith?"

"Your h-home? This evening?"

"What's wrong? You can come, can't you?"

"Uh, yes, ma'am, I can come. I was just thinking about, uh, the homework you assigned earlier."

"Well, you'll just have to double up tonight in order to try harder. Diagramming thentences can be a lot of fun once you know how to recognize mithplaced or dangling modifiers. You do know what a dangling modifier ith, don't you?"

"Uh, that's like having a big, long participle, isn't it?

"Er...yeah, right," she said and looked at me kind of funny, like she knew what I was really trying to say.

"Tommy, what about thith evening about..."

"Five thirty?"

"Yeth, five thirty will be fine. Oh, remember to bring your book."

"Yes, ma'am! Books...five-thirty...this evening," I said and grabbed my books and raced for the door.

I couldn't wait to get home to start getting ready for Miss Maze. At five o'clock, I was fully dressed and ready to go; however, I didn't want my folks to get too suspicious. After I showered, I put on a clean pair of underwear, keeping on my same school clothes. I also splashed some of Dad's Old Spice cologne over my face. Then I cheerfully told my folks I was going to help Bo build a science project for Biology. Little did they know the project was Miss Maze. In order to make good on my story, I stopped by Bo's to tell him not to call my house tonight.

At five-thirty sharp, I was on her doorstep. Although I was a little nervous, I was geared up to see Miss Maze. I decided it would be more macho not to act surprised but to be prepared for anything.

"Who ith it?"

"It's Tommy, Miss Maze. I'm here for my lessons!" I shouted from the doorstep.

"Oh, I'll be right there."

When the door opened, there stood Miss Maze. She was wearing the same skirt-n-blouse she'd had on at school. I looked past her to see if I could see any lit candles or hear any soft music playing. Nothing!

"Come on in, Tommy. I just got in from the thtore. My, I thee you remembered to bring your book. You seem excited to get thtarted?"

"Yes, ma'am."

"I was getting ready to have a cup of hot tea. Would you like a cup?"

"Some tea?"

"Yeth, ith herb tea with lemon and honey. I like my tea thweet," she said with a big smile.

"Sure, I love tea!" I said, trying not to look disappointed.

"Okay. By the way, did your parents mention anything about your coming over thith evening?"

"Uh, they didn't say much of anything. I'm sure they think it's a good idea for me to learn new things."

"Oh, well have a theat at the table and I'll get the tea. Then we'll get right to work."

When Miss Maze went into the kitchen, my eyes scanned her house for a real good looking over. She kept a very neat home. Everything looked organized and nicely decorated. A white leather couch sat on the floor in the living room; nearby was a matching loveseat with two antique chairs. A huge bookshelf stacked with old books, miniature vases, and a glass unicorn flanked the right of the couch. On the left was a small table with a brass lamp. The floor was covered with a blue, expensive-looking carpet. On a wall near the loveseat hung a picture of a man, a woman, and three children. I took a closer look at the picture, realizing it must have been a family portrait. One of the children was Miss Maze, and she looked to have been about 15. Gosh, she was beautiful even then.

Miss Maze walked back in with the tea, and I sat down at the table. I watched her pour her tea first and then start to pour mine. She still smelled good when she was up close to me. When she began to pour my tea, I asked her about the picture on the living room wall. As she spun around to see which picture I was referring to, she missed my cup and poured hot tea on my lap.

"Owww!" I screamed and bolted up from the table. It looked like I had peed in my pants.

"Oh, Tommy I'm tho thorry. Here, let me wipe you off."

Miss Maze ran to the kitchen, grabbed a towel, got down on her knees and started wiping the wet spot on my pants. All the while wiping and apologizing, she said, "Oh, Tommy, I'm tho thorry. Here, go into the bathroom and take off those wet panth. I'll throw them in the dryer. You can use my bathrobe in there until your panth dry. I'm tho thorry."

"No problem," I said, trying to sound cool. I went into the bathroom, slipped out of my jeans and held them out the door to Miss Maze for her to put in the dryer. I could still hear Miss Maze saying how sorry she was as she was walking away from the door. Once I was inside the bathroom, I realized how stupid this whole idea had been.

"Tommy, you alright in there? Doth the robe fit?"

"Uh, yes, ma'am. It fits good. I'll be right out."

I hurriedly pulled on the pink bathrobe, wrapped myself up, and walked out to face Miss Maze.

"It fits well," she corrected me. "It fits good is not proper English, Tommy."

"Yes, ma'am."

"You look very good in pink, Tommy," she teased. "Come on, leth finith our tea."

"Aw right," I said as we walked to her kitchen and sat down at her table. I had to walk slowly to keep the robe from coming open. I carefully drank my tea without looking directly at Miss Maze and without making any conversation.

"Okay, time for your lesson, Tommy. Where do you think you need the most help?"

"Where?"

"I mean, which area of English? Nouns, verbs, clauses, participles?"

"Oh, uh, I could use some help with my participle. I'm not sure how it works."

"You mean participles, don't you? Okay, take out a sheet of paper and let's get to work," she said and reached in her bookbag for her textbook.

When she bent down, I caught a quick glimpse of her cleavage. Her perfume penetrated my nostrils and made me dizzy, in a good kind of way.

"A *participle* functions like a verb and a modifier," she read. "It modifies an ancillary; thus, it functions as an adjective."

"What's an ancillary?"

"Ancillary means an auxiliary function or to work as an aid to another word," she said and moved closer to me, as if wanting to demonstrate on me with her hands. "A participle modifies by describing the ancillary as performing or receiving action, or existing in a state of being; thus, it functions as a verb."

"Oh, I see."

"Do you really understand, Tommy?"

"No, ma'am, I mean, yes, ma'am, I understand. Really."

"Then give me a thentence using a participle."

"Okay, but can you jumpstart me with an example first?"

"Sure. Here's one: 'The *beating* waves dashed against the rocks.' The participle *beating* describes the waves as performing the action of beating. Now you try one."

"Aw right, that's easy. Uh, 'My beating heart smashed against the rocks.'"

"Oh, that was very good, Tommy. You did very well."

"Can we try another one, Miss Maze, please?"

"Sure, Tommy. You really are excited tonight. If only you could do thith in clath, your grade would be much better."

She gave me three more sentences, which I got all right. We moved on to verbs, nouns, adverbs, and run-ons. All night she told me how brilliant I was. I was on a roll. And then it happened.

"Uh-oh. Will you excuse me for a moment, Tommy? I turned my computer on but I forgot to print my lesson plans for tomorrow," she said and quickly disappeared into a back room. Was this it? I was convinced this was the move and her way of letting me know she was ready. So was I.

I loosened the pink bathrobe on me a little to appear sexier, and I sniffed myself to see if Dad's Old Spice was still there. It was. I then dimmed the lights and moved over to the white leather loveseat and waited. In order to feel more relaxed, I put my feet on her coffee table, slouched back on one of the pillows, and yawned really wide. The next thing I heard was a soft, sexy voice whispering in my ear, "Tommy, are you athleep ...Tommy?" My eyes shot open, and there stood Mandy. She had apparently dimmed the lights a little more because I could barely see her body, but I could see enough to know that it was her.

"I could tell what you've been thinking."

"Uh, huh."

"Well, what are you waiting for? Take off the robe and lie back on the *love seat* and let me give you a nice matthage."

"Okay, Miss Maze..."

"Please, Tommy, call me Mandy."

"What you gonna do with that big buzzy thing?"

"It's a matthage wand. I'm going to give you a matthage all over."

"All over? You mean everywhere?"

"Yeth, everywhere, and then you can do me. Now turn over."

I turned over on my stomach and let her run that thing over my shoulders and then down my back. When she got too close to my tush, I started screaming.

"Tommy, what's the matter? I heard you all the way in the other room."

I opened my eyes and saw Miss Maze standing over me, shaking me. She was fully dressed in the same clothes she had on before she left the room.

"You must have fallen athleep and had a bad dream. And I was only gone for a minute. I think ith time for you to go home. We can finith thith at school."

"No, no, Miss Maze, please. I don't want to go home yet. I want to..."

"Tommy, don't be thilly. I'll get your panth out of the dryer and you can get drethed, okay?"

"Okay."

She walked out of the room and came back in a minute with my jeans. I said, "Thank you" and I went to change. I hurried up, got dressed and headed out the bathroom door.

"Uh, Miss Maze, could you please write a note to my dad and tell him how well I did tonight? He'll want to know my progress," I said with a grin.

"Why, sure, Tommy. What's your father's name?"

"Bo."

"Bo? Ith that hith real name?

"Uh, yes ma'am, just Bo. He doesn't like to be called Mr."

"Okay, what do you want me to write?"

"Just say, 'Dear Bo, Tommy was very good tonight, and I'll be glad to help him with his dangling participles and other stuff anytime he needs it.'"

Miss Maze must have been exhausted because she didn't argue. She took my pen and wrote the note just as I had dictated it. Before she could comment, I grabbed the note, ran for the door, and yelled, "Thanks, Miss Maze, for a wonderful evening."

"Good evening, Tommy."

# THE BAPTIST BOTTOM BOYS

Once upon a time, doo-wop was king. This was long before rock rolled into town and onto the musical scene. Street-corner symphonies were the order of the day in the early 1950s but mostly at night, as scores of teenagers lined the streets to sing or *blow harmonies*, as they called it then. For some neighborhoods, musical instruments were scarce, so everything heard on the corners was a cappella – without any musical instruments other than a trash can for a drum or a stick banging on a pole to keep time. Neighborhoods all over the world had budding young singers who sought fame and fortune using their self-taught talents. Groups sprang up virtually overnight, and many of them went on to create musical history. From around the country, names like The Tams, The Ravens, The Drifters, The Flamingos, The Dells, The Doves, The Coasters, The Cadillacs, The Moonglows, and many, many more all began singing a cappella on neighborhood streetcorners just like the ones found in the Baptist Bottom in my hometown.

The Baptist Bottom was not a place where people wanted to live or raise their kids. Some may have called it a ghetto, but it was home to many good people who were poor in money but enormously wealthy with God-given talents. From an aerial view, the Bottom looked like a small, squared-off area that only contained a few dirty street corners and several shabby buildings. At close range, the two most prominent or notable buildings were a shingle-laced, wooden funeral home and a red-bricked Baptist church. Centerstone Baptist Church, located in the midst of the Bottom, was the reason the area got its name. For years, the graffiti-laden buildings around the church served as the backdrop to all of the amateur doo-wop groups that gathered to sing. Doo-wop was raw, original, untapped talent, and every town had talent shows to seek out the best. There were many groups that started out well but later broke up before doo-wop became big. A lot of these groups started by singing gospel during church revivals and later switched over. And when they sang, they really set the churches on fire with large crowds gathering to hear them.

It was 1957 when the talent show of all talent shows put the Baptist Bottom on the map. Every weekend was special to the teenagers who crammed the corners to dance and sing, but one particular Saturday night would be very special for a group called Jolly and the Overtones. The soulful preliminaries took place on Friday night on the corner of West North Street and Lena Avenue. There were no official judges as the winners were selected by the applause of the street audience. By eight o'clock Saturday night, the crowd had reduced the competition to only five groups. The lineup finale included the best and most consistent acts throughout the competing neighborhoods. From Cooper Street, The Loveletters reigned supreme. Willie Times and the Tick Tocks represented Seeger Drive, and The Barrettes, an all-girl group, was the best from the Lake Street area. A relatively new group, The Hoops, defended the notorious Fordham Avenue, and Jolly and the Overtones was the pride of West North Street, better known as the Baptist Bottom.

Eliga Reynolds was nicknamed Jolly because of his rotund appearance and his big smile. He had an uncanny but natural ability to sing and write songs. Jolly was athletic and a good dancer too. His paper-sack brown complexion and short wavy hair made most girls think he was very cute and as cuddly as a stuffed teddy. If doo-wop was king, then Jolly was the crowned prince of a cappella. Jolly and his group were by far the best doo-wop group around, and they had been together since the tenth grade. These cats could really sing, and it was generally accepted that if a group could sing a cappella without a band, then they were destined to be stars one day. Jolly's silky-sweet falsetto blended magically with the Overtones' wild and crazy harmonized antics to create an unusual sound but a most electrifying act. Jolly wrote most of the group's songs, and a lot of them were pretty good. He was always working on a new song and a new way to represent the best of the Baptist Bottom. Their self-penned songs like "Wishing at the Well of Love" and "Stars in my Heart" made them guaranteed winners at most of the talent shows.

Jolly's best friends from school and the Baptist Bottom area were The Overtones. They included Robert "Bay-T" Neal (first tenor); Clifford "Pro-Duce" Rich (bass); Kenneth "Chappie" Rumph (baritone); and Wendell "Tadpole" Potter (second tenor). Each was blessed with a natural singing ability, an innate sense of rhythm and timing, and a good sense of humor. They each had unique characteristics, too. Bay-T was the undisputed clown of the group. Chappie was the quiet, shy one. Pro-Duce and Tadpole were the best dancers; they were tall and lanky, and they gave the group a polished, professional look when they swayed and popped their fingers. Although each member was capable of handling lead, Jolly had that extra-added charm to stand out front, make the group look good, and make the audience feel great. At times, Bay-T would co-lead a song with Jolly, but normally it was Jolly all the way. From the beginning, it was unanimously decided that Jolly would sing lead. And the group liked it that way, because when Jolly was at his best, the group was at its best. He somehow injected energy into the group with every note he crooned. During one performance, Jolly held a high note for record length as the audience loudly counted out the number of seconds like a boxing referee during a knockdown. Not many singers, amateur or otherwise, could hold a note for forty-eight seconds, but Jolly did, and he still had enough wind left to finish the song with his usual silky-sweet smoothness.

During the talent show, each group got the chance to sing three selections before the next group could perform. The Loveletters started first with an unusually melodic rendition of The Flamingos' "I Only Have Eyes for You." Near the end of the song, each of the members echoed a soft, whispery "you" while pointing to the girls in the audience. This little stunt never failed to reap loud screams and yells from the crowd, especially the girls. They maintained their momentum by following up with another pretty ballad, and they concluded with an exceptional version of "Sincerely" made famous by Harvey and the Moonglows.

Willie Times and the Tick Tocks had a more lukewarm reception, partly because of the songs they selected and partly because their bass singer sounded hoarse. He worked as one of those guys who yelled *ALL ABOARD!* down at the train depot and when the time came for him to hit a deep note, he sounded more like a soprano. Friday night was a much better night for Willie Times and his group. The crowd politely applauded so that the group wouldn't feel discouraged. However, as they walked away from the center spot, one wise guy in the audience couldn't resist giving them the official basketball hand gesture that meant Time Out.

By the time The Barrettes came on, the excitement was again high. The performance of an all-girl group was not rare, and when the girls were good *and* good-looking, it typically made the boys in the crowd go crazy with wolf calls. And The Barrettes were as good and good-looking as they came.

The group consisted of two sisters and a cousin; all three had lovely pecan-tan complexions and long, curly hair, which was worn in ponytails and fastened with large, red barrettes. Each girl was about five-foot-four and weighed no more than one hundred pounds. As far as their singing, most guys thought they were well-rounded and fully developed. Julie, the lead singer, began with a song that had more of a Sunday morning gospel feel; these kinds of songs were sure to arouse the soulful mood of the crowd. Later, Teresa and Hilda joined Julie for their last two numbers, both up-tempo and complete with fancy foot-stomping, hand-clapping, and harmonic background vocals. The guys reciprocated with wolf-whistles and shouts of "Sang, Baby, Sang!"

Next, it was time for the new group, The Hoops. It was customary for the reigning favorite group to perform last; however, Jolly and the Overtones were not displaying their usual coolness and confidence about winning. They appeared expressionless as they quietly watched the groups perform before them. The Hoops had only been together for a few months, but they had each been members of other groups. They actually looked more like a basketball team than a singing group since each of them was over six feet. It was assumed that their group name was derived from the game of basketball or, as someone jokingly suggested, from whooping cranes. The Hoops boasted three featured lead singers and each was supposed to be a master of a particular song. Out first, Billy Pruett sang a smooth, soothing tenor rendition of the Ink Spots' "If I Didn't Care." The cat sang so cool and confident that the crowd almost forgot that the group had two more songs to sing. The crowd was awed. Next, Anthony Willis' falsetto cover of "Tenderly" garnered even louder applause. Two out of three was pretty good for a new group. Everyone was surprised, including Jolly. Willis' voice was strong, clear, and sounded just as good as Jolly's, if not better. Last, Willeen Cole, bass, sang a misplaced but stirring rendition of "Precious Lord." Never had the crowd heard such talent from a new group. The Hoops had just made it tough for anyone to follow them, including the remaining favorite act.

All eyes were now on Jolly and the Overtones. Someone from the crowd teasingly announced, "And now, the world-famous, Baptist Bottom Boys, er, I mean, Jolly and the Overtones!" The crowd snickered for a moment then immediately hushed as Pro-Duce pushed through to make his way out front. Closely behind him were Tadpole, Bay-T, and Chappie. The members positioned themselves in their usual formation and started to snap their fingers for time and rhythm. With the group snapping in rhythm, Pro-Duce took a step up and began to deliver a deep, preachy monologue.

"Folks, we'd like to begin tonight by singing a new song written by our lead singer. However, he won't be singing lead on this one. This song will feature our baritone, Kenneth 'Chappie' Rumph." The crowd then realized Jolly was missing from the lineup, but before the audience had time to react, Chappie's velvety baritone began crooning the lyrics to their new song, "Romeo Without Juliet."

> Oh, Romeo without Juliet
> Is a love I'll never forget
> For I understand now how he felt
> Losing a love his heart still kept.

> I'm no Romeo but I love you
> And I hope you know it's true
> Girl, wherefore art thou, I say
> Won't you please come back to stay.

> Beneath your balcony of love, I stand
> Waiting for you to take my hand
> My life is over if you don't return
> That's a lesson I don't want to learn.

> Oh, Romeo without Juliet
> Is a love I'll never forget
> For I understand now how he felt
> Losing a love his heart still kept.

Together with background vocals that accented every rhyme, Bay-T, Tadpole, and Pro-Duce joined in to make this new song an unprecedented doo-wop classic in style and harmony. The crowd had never heard much from the other guys in the group, and that made the Overtones hotter and more intriguing than the newly discovered Hoops. Even the groups that performed earlier were seen applauding.

127

Chappie sheepishly beamed and smiled as the crowd lifted him up away from the group.

"Man, that was a bad piece," exclaimed one guy. "Jolly may have written it, but you sang the dew right off that one, man." Throughout all the commotion, all Chappie could be heard saying was "thank you, thank you."

Suddenly, Jolly appeared from behind the crowd and joined the group. With all the thrill and rapture of the moment, Jolly seemed readier than ever to perform. After the crowd returned Chappie back to the center, the group was ready to perform its second number. The crowd quieted down, and again, Pro-Duce stepped out front and coolly announced another surprise in their repertoire.

"Folks, this next song will feature Bay-T. It's one we hope you'll enjoy," said Pro-Duce as he looked around at the unpredictable Bay-T. Astonished, the crowd now wondered if Jolly was going to sing at all. After Chappie had ignited the fire and received such a big hoopla, Bay-T was ready and he didn't want to take any chances. He wanted to keep the fire burning, so he looked around at the guys, snapped his fingers, and whispered, "Let's do 'In the Still of the Night.'" From the first word that came from his a cappella mouth, the audience popped its fingers and rocked along with Bay-T. "In The Still of the Night" never sounded better, with Pro-Duce adding a mean bass to complement Bay-T's eloquent tenor. The audience's applause seemed to signify that it had already given the show to the Overtones. There was only one more song for the group to sing, and the crowd suspected that Jolly would be the dessert or the icing on the cake.

Being in last place was the edge that the Overtones had used to position themselves to win. They had closely observed the other groups and strategically decided that the best way to win would be to combine the best of all the groups' little skits with their own unique style but do it better – that way, they couldn't lose. They planned to show The Hoops that they, too, had more than one lead singer; they'd prove to The Barrettes that they could arouse and move the crowd too; they would demonstrate to The Loveletters that they could be sweet, romantic, and awesome; and finally, they would let Willie Times in on their "secret" of how a bass singer should really sound.

When the crowd finally quieted down, Pro-Duce was back out front for his last monologue. This time he kept it short because he knew Jolly needed no introduction. He simply said, "And here's Jolly." The crowd whistled and cheered. The new all-cotton pullover that Jolly wore was a little too big; he had bought it for the show and was hoping it would later shrink after being washed. At least it kept his stomach from looking like it was hanging over his beltline. As he walked out front, his teenage voice softly announced that he was going to sing a song made famous by Miss Billie Holiday. The crowd didn't respond – not because of disapproval, but because it couldn't readily associate Billie Holiday with doo-wop. However, the unwritten rule of talent shows is for the audience to suspend its judgment until after the group has finished. Before Jolly started, he added, "Er, we re-arranged this song a little to make it fit the sound of the Baptist Bottom. The name of the song is 'Solitude.'" As Jolly began to sing, he thought how good Anthony Willis' falsetto had sounded. With that in mind, he sang with a new power to emulate Willis' voice. There was no contest. Jolly made Billie's song a doo-wop favorite from that night on. Other groups even included it in their repertoire, but no one could do it like Jolly and the Overtones. The audience applauded wildly, almost riot-like. The way Jolly phrased the song's lyrics and held the high notes was outstanding. Near the end of the song, the Overtones decided to mock The Loveletters by softly echoing the word *solitude*. But instead of pointing their fingers at the crowd, they choreographed a quick dance step, slid back, folded their arms, looked at Jolly, and pointed at him as he sang his last words. In his highest, clearest, and prettiest falsetto, Jolly escalated, "In…my…SOLITUDE!"

It took all of ten minutes for the crowd to calm down. The crowd encircled all five members and proceeded to lift them up one by one while chanting, "Overtones, Overtones, Overtones!" It took three boys to lift Jolly, but he too was uplifted and hailed. The crowd then singled out Jolly and focused on his name alone, yelling, "Jolly, Jolly, Jolly!"

The proprietors of Happ's Grill and Grissley's Barber Shop could be seen peering out their windows, wondering exactly what was going on. They were used to the kids singing in the streets, but they'd never heard this kind of commotion before. Mr. Grissley even came outside and yelled, "You boys better quit that fighting out there, or I'll call the cops!" One of the teenagers yelled back, "Man, we ain't fighting. The Overtones just blowed away everybody at the show. And they wuz bad, too!" As old man Grissley began to walk back inside, he turned and shouted back, "Overtones my foot. Y'all better TONE down some of that fuss!" But nothing or no one could chill the ecstasy of The Overtones' sweet victory. Although the unofficial prize given to them by someone in the crowd was five dollars and a pat on the back, it was quite obvious to everyone present that Jolly and the Overtones had won much more that night.

While walking home together after the talent show, Jolly and the group joyously reflected on everyone's performance.

"Man, did y'all hear how deep Pro-Duce's voice was when he said, 'Folks, we'd like to begin tonight by singing a new song'?" mimicked Bay-T.

"Yeah, I thought he was going to say ALL-A-ABOARD any minute. Hey, maybe Pro-Duce can apply for a job down at the train depot," Chappie said, laughing.

"But did y'all see The Barrettes? Man, that Teresa is built better than a brick outhouse. Ain't she?" said Bay-T.

"Naw, man, I think Julie is the cutest. She's got the prettiest eyes and the sweetest voice," argued Pro-Duce.

"Pro-Duce, I keep telling you that eyes and voice ain't got nothing to do with it. I'm talking about her body, man. I could care less if she could see or sing," said Bay-T.

"I thought The Hoops were pretty good, but they sure seemed upset that they didn't win tonight. They wouldn't even shake our hands," reflected Chappie.

"That's cause they're from Fordham Avenue. You know that neighborhood has a reputation for hotheads," Tadpole said.

"And what about the look on The Loveletters' faces when we cut that little step and then pointed at Jolly?" asked Pro-Duce.

"Yeah, I bet they thought Jolly was going to miss that high note and sing off-key," giggled Bay-T.

"Actually, I was sort of afraid I might miss it, too. Anthony Willis was very good tonight. His voice was clear and...."

"But you were better," interrupted Tadpole.

"We were all good," continued Jolly. "Especially you guys. You know, I was thinking. Maybe we should change our name to just The Overtones. I wouldn't mind at all. I can still write songs, and we can all take turns singing lead."

The rest of the group became silent, and no one would speak until Bay-T broke the silence with, "Since I was so good tonight, why not change the name to Bay-T and the Overtones?"

"I was better than you," teased Chappie. "What's wrong with Chappie and the Overtones?"

Jolly, Pro-Duce, and Tadpole all laughed and continued to walk home, leaving Bay-T and Chappie to continue their make-believe fight. Everyone realized that Bay-T had saved the day with his timely humor, for the group really didn't want to discuss changing its name or its lead, ever. They knew Jolly was special and that his being out front had more to do with just singing. He was their leader and their friend, which was a major source of pride for them.

Bay-T and Chappie soon caught up, and everything was again back to normal. To keep things that way, Chappie began singing

"Romeo Without Juliet" and, as usual, the rest joined in. They finished the song just as they reached the crest of a concrete mound. Things were again silent for a second, but again, Bay-T changed all that.

"Hey, let's divvy up the five bucks so I can buy me a new wardrobe. I still think Bay-T and the Overtones has a nice ring to it," Bay-T said with his familiar, wide Cheshire Cat grin.

In the distance, a loud roar of laughter could be heard as five silhouetted figures, now flanked by clouds, the moon, and stars, danced out of sight. The story that had just taken place near the center of an illegitimate but proud neighborhood was cinematic or larger than life. The music world outside this place may have never known the name Jolly and the Overtones, but Eliga, Clifford, Kenneth, Wendell, and Robert will forever be known as the Baptist Bottom Boys.

# "THE PINK TREE HOUSE"

veryone loves tree houses. They seem to make us feel big when we're smaller and when we get older and bigger, they magically make us feel smaller all over again. Our imagination and our dreams take pleasure in knowing that we are safe living high above inside our own little perfect world built just for us. But when it comes to tree houses, girls have never been quite equal to boys it seems. There was no time or place in history where this was truer than in my hometown when I was growing up. I still remember that awful sign posted on my brother's ugly tree house that read:

## "NO GIRLS ALLOWED, KEEP OUT!"

It was during the summer when school was not in session. My brother Jay and his two geeky friends, Bug and Squirrel, ruined one of the trees in our backyard with scrap wood, cardboard boxes, bicycle tires, rope, plastic and anything else they could find to make their silly tree-high club house. This tree house was an eyesore to everyone else but Jay loved it – mainly because he considered it a safe haven that was off-limits to girls, especially me, his sister Fay. Their tree house was shabby with cardboard walls and a plywood floor. The roof was no better as it was made out of scrap wood with holes. When it rained, they looked stupid sitting up there with umbrellas to keep from getting wet. At times it was laughable at how dumb boys could be, especially when they were trying to be coy. Jay was trying to impress my friend Mae Ruth and Squirrel had a crush on my friend Tootie. No girls liked Bug because he looked just like his name. The boys naturally thought that tree houses were meant only for them – they figured girls couldn't climb trees, swing on ropes, and weren't smart enough to construct their own tree houses.

Mae Ruth, Tootie and I set out to prove them wrong. We planned to construct our own tree house about 50 yards away from theirs. Since we lived way out in the country, we had a huge backyard with plenty of trees. Our folks didn't seem to mind us playing in the trees as long as we didn't cut them down. Without giving away our scheme, we'd plan to canvass the neighborhood to see how much materials and support we could get to build our tree house.

The three of us decided to put our plan in motion around midday one Friday. The boys were out back playing their disgusting little watermelon seed-spitting contest. They had invented this game where two of the boys would gulp a handful of freshly-spat watermelon seeds and then spit them across a finish line to see who could spit the farthest. The third boy would serve as the referee and the judge to decide who won at the other end. The winning prize was usually a nickel or a dime. The last time Jay won, I paid dearly when I noticed many of the watermelon seeds he had gulped came out in his dookie when he went to the bathroom. I went to the bathroom behind him and realized he either forgot to flush or did not flush on purpose so that I would see them. Brothers can be so gross and disgusting at times.

Our first stop was at the home of Mrs. Gertrude, the neighborhood seamstress and clothes designer. She'd been making clothes for as long as anyone knew; she used to work in a big department store downtown where she did all their clothing alterations. When we got to her house, she was sitting on her porch swing sipping lemonade and admiring her roses. She was in her 70's and now a spry retiree; her new passion was tending her roses, which were the best and prettiest in town.

"Hi Mrs. Gertrude," we all said in unison. "We love your roses."

"Hey girls. Thank you. Ya'll out for the summer?"

"Yes ma'am," I said. "We're working on a project and we come to ask you for some advice," I added as we all walked up on her porch, being careful not to get pricked by a thorn from a rose bush close to her swing.

"What kind of project?"

"We're planning to build a tree house," Mae Ruth blurted.

"You mean a doll house, don't you?"

"No, we mean a tree house. We're going to build our own tree house, but better than my brother's," I said. "They won't let us girls play in theirs."

Mrs. Gertrude sat there and studied each of us for a minute as she took a big sip of her lemonade. She had always been known to be a defender of women. Then she said, "I've designed all kinds of clothes for people but I haven't ever designed a tree house. It might be fun. Let's go inside and see what we girls can do."

After spending about an hour inside Mrs. Getrtrude's home, we came out running with one of her drawings on a piece of paper. We were filled with lemonade and ideas. She had given us a pattern that she thought would make a perfect tree house for girls. The only materials she promised to give us were lace and cloth for the inside window curtains of our tree house. Mrs. Gertrude also suggested we go see Mr. Mackie, the neighborhood junk dealer, for additional supplies. She waved as we rushed off to follow her advice.

Our next stop was at the home of Mr. Mackie. He always had a lot of neat stuff lying around in his backyard. Of course, Mackie wasn't his real name but the whole town called him that for some reason; sometimes he wore lipstick, make-up and women's wigs but he was a nice man. He actually preferred to be called Mackie so we called him that too, but our parents made us put the word "Mr." in front to show respect. I knocked on his front door while Tootie and Mae Ruth looked around in his yard to spot some things we might want in our tree house.

"Hold on, I'm coming," said Mr. Mackie as he approached his door.

"Hi, Mr. Mackie. It's me, Mae Ruth and Tootie."

"Hey Fay and girls. What ya'll need?"

"We plan to build a tree house and we need some materials. We didn't know what all we'll need so Mrs. Gertrude suggested we come ask you for some help."

"A tree house... what kind of tree house... for girls?"

"Yes," said Tootie. "We can build one too if we had the stuff. We already have an idea of how it should look," she added while showing him Mrs. Gertrude's pattern. His long fingers delicately caressed the paper and brought it in close to the thick glasses on his nose; I thought it was funny how Mr. Mackie's nose kissed the paper as he looked at the design. His lips were still moist and pink from the lipstick he had been wearing before he came to the door.

"Come on in and let's look out back to see what I got," he said as he gently handed the paper back to Tootie. Mr. Mackie now looked perplexed but amused at the same time.

As soon as we walked outside into his backyard, we saw mounds and mounds of neat stuff, known to everyone else as just junk. Mr. Mackie regarded his stuff as merchandise that he would sell to anyone who needed it the most. Mae Ruth pointed to a big, old picture frame and Tootie spotted a wooden apple box that would make a fine table for our tree house. I saw a palette of wood planks that would make a good ladder to get up to our tree house. Mr. Mackie showed us some cans of left over paint that he had stacked on the side of his house; the only two colors he had left were red and white. He gave us an old wheelbarrow to carry our materials back to our tree. After spending about thirty minutes in Mr. Mackie's backyard, we had accumulated enough materials to get started on our building project. Mr. Mackie seemed happy to have helped us and told us to thank Mrs. Gertrude for sending us over. He also told us to come back anytime if we needed any more stuff. We thanked Mr. Mackie profusely and starting making our way back home, all of us girls pushing the wobbly wheelbarrow in an effort to make it easier.

When we got back home, we pushed the wheelbarrow into the barn and covered it over with hay to keep our secret hidden a little longer while we figured out our next steps. We didn't want Jay and his friends to uncover our plot and make fun of us just yet; however, they rarely ever played in the barn anyway.

"You think we got enough stuff to build our tree house?" Mae Ruth asked.

"I don't think so. We still need some stuff for the roof, the walls and the floors," I answered.

"My dad and brothers work down at the lumber yard. We can ask them for some wood," said Tootie.

"That's a great idea, Tootie. Let's ask them."

Tootie's brothers volunteered to bring some old wood planks from the lumber yard to our barn. Later that day they brought a truckload of wood over and helped stack it in the barn near the other stuff; her brothers also loaned us a bucket full of nails, some hammers and a hand saw. The three of us now felt we had enough materials to get started. Tootie took out Mrs. Gertrude's pattern and laid it on the ground so we all could look at it; she suggested we paint the wood planks for the walls, floors and roof before we hammered them together. Tootie said that way we wouldn't have to climb the ladder to paint them after the tree house was built. We all thought that made good sense. We took out the cans of paint and tried to decide if we wanted our tree house to be white with red trim or red with white trim since those were our only two choices. Then Mae Ruth said, "Why don't we mix the two colors together? In art class we learned how to mix primary colors together to make other colors. We can mix red and white to make pink."

"Wow, a pink tree house? That's another good idea," I said.

Excited about getting started on our pink tree house, we borrowed three of daddy's old paint brushes from inside the barn. We found an empty paint can and poured in some of the red paint and then the white paint, stirring it with a stick to mix it properly. Then we started painting the wood planks pink. We figured they'd be dry by Saturday morning so we could get started building our tree house. I knew then Jay and his friends would be swimming at the local pool.

Early Saturday morning we met up at the barn to start our construction. First we hammered the pink planks together for the ladder and ran it up to the first big branch of the tree. After that we measured the distance between the tree branches and then started sawing some wood to make a foundation for the floor, all the while looking at Mrs. Gertrude's pattern. Tootie and I climbed up in the tree while Mae Ruth handed us the sawed wood for the floor. We took turns getting up in the tree until each of us had a chance to hammer nails into what would be our floor. Once we had the floor finished, we kept on hammering wood together until we had one of the walls in place. About four hours had gone by before our project started to really resemble a house. Mae Ruth figured out how to put a window into one of the walls without having to cut out a square; she used the big picture frame we got from Mr. Mackie's and called it a picture window. Before long we had the floor and all four walls in place. Since we did not have enough wood to make an angled roof, we decided to make a flat roof instead. The last thing we made was a sliding panel front door to our tree house. After ten hours of planning, painting, sawing, and hammering, we had completed our project; our tree house was big enough to hold about six and it was sturdy. We climbed down the ladder and looked up at our pink tree house – something we girls had built all by ourselves. We couldn't wait for everyone to see it now.

Over the next few hours, we decorated the interior with knick-knacks we got from here and there. Tootie brought an old piece of carpet and laid it on top of the wooden floor. She also brought a small cooler with snacks inside. Mae Ruth brought fresh flowers from her mother's garden; we stuck them in soda pop bottles and called them flower vases. I found some old Christmas tree lights in our attic and strung them around the top, although they were not connected to an electrical outlet. Tootie brought a flashlight for when it got dark. We even got Mrs. Gertrude to make a simple cloth and lace curtain for the one big picture window. The apple box was our centerpiece table and it had a multi-purpose use; we could play cards on it, eat on it, or sit on it if we wanted to. We placed a hand-painted sign above the door that read:

### "WELCOME TO OUR PINK TREE HOUSE!"

Later on that day, Jay and his two friends showed up. They immediately started laughing and pointing to our tree house while hurling all kinds of insults.

"Hey guys, do you see what I see? Somebody must have built a tree house for my cry baby sister and her friends," said Jay.

"Looks like it was built by a fairy," said Squirrel. "It's pink. Whoever heard of a pink tree house?"

"I think it actually looks kinda neat," said Bug, looking up in disbelief.

"No, it doesn't. Bug, are you crazy? It looks weird and girly."

"Jay, you're just jealous 'cause it looks better than yours. Besides, we didn't need nobody to build it for us… we built it ourselves," Mae Ruth snapped.

What Mae Ruth said stopped Jay dead in his tracks and caused him to just look dumb with his mouth wide open.

"That's right," added Tootie. "We built it ourselves. And we got the blue print to prove it," she said as she showed them Mrs. Gertrude's drawing.

I didn't have to say a word after that. I just stood there smiling and enjoying the look on their faces when they finally realized that we girls did build it ourselves and it did look better than theirs.

"But how? Where did you get all the stuff?"

"That's for us to know and you to find out Jay" I blurted.

"Can I see inside?" asked Bug, smiling and looking at me.

"Sure, if you want," I answered. Then I watched Bug as he quickly climbed the pink ladder and stuck his head inside our tree house.

"Wow, guys it's neat inside. They have it decorated and all. They even have carpet, a table and a picture window with curtains."

"I wanna see next," said Squirrel as he waved for Bug to climb down so he could go up too.

I could see Jay steaming as he watched his excited pals suddenly switch over to our side with amazement and compliments. He tried to remain calm but the curiosity was killing him; he wanted to look inside also but was too stubborn to ask.

"Jay, you wanna go up?" asked Mae Ruth. She then smiled and grabbed his hand. "I'll go up with you if you want."

"Why don't we all go up? It's big enough to hold six," I said, saving the day for my brother. It was clear that Mae Ruth liked Jay too. Like I said, at times it was laughable at how dumb boys could be.

Once we got inside, there was a cool breeze blowing and the window curtains moved as we sat quietly. It was getting to be dusk and the full moon was shining through our picture window. At first there was an awkward feeling in the air but then Tootie reached inside her little cooler and offered soda pops to everyone. She clicked on the flashlight and sat it on top of the apple box so that it shone up on the ceiling, illuminating the inside of the tree house. After everyone had a drink, she reached back inside the cooler and pulled out some Moon Pies – both chocolate and vanilla. "Moon Pies for a full moon," she joked. We shared the Moon Pies by breaking them in half to make sure we each got some of both. Soon after that talking and laughter could be heard throughout the tree house. Squirrel sat next to Tootie, Mae Ruth sat next to Jay, and Bug sat next to me. The closer I sat to him made me realize that Bug really didn't look all that bad. In fact, he was kind of cute, in a buggish kind of way.

I can't explain it but somehow after we built the pink tree house, we all became closer, especially Jay and me. We didn't fight as much and he even started flushing the toilet after he used it. The word about our pink tree house quickly spread throughout the neighborhood. The next day at church Reverend Higgins preached about the *Tree of Life* – we took that as his nod to us that even he knew about our pink tree house. The Bible doesn't mention tree houses but Reverend Higgins did say how valuable trees are in our lives; he was right because our lives did sort of revolve around the tree house after it was built. The tree house became a central focus in our lives and it connected all of us to each other. Every other girl in town now wanted one too. Most of the boys who wanted to get close to girls smartened up and offered to help the girls construct their tree houses, making it a joint boy-girl project.

A few weeks after we built our tree house, a big storm came and destroyed Jay's tree house but ours remained intact. Instead of getting mad, he laughed and said it was nothing but a big eyesore anyway. We offered to help him build another one but he refused, saying he liked ours better; that was a big admission for Jay and it meant he must have been maturing. Over the years the sun lightened the pink paint on ours but the structure remained solid. That was many years ago. Most of the people like Mrs. Gertrude and Mr. Mackie, who were associated with the construction of our tree house have either died or moved away. Years later I found Mrs. Gertrude's drawing of our tree house in a box I had packed; I will always be indebted to her and Mr. Mackie for their kindness and support, and I will never forget them.

As they got older, Jay and Mae Ruth went out on some dates; they even went to their senior prom together. After high school Squirrel and Tootie attended the same college. Squirrel became a star football player and Tootie majored in Construction Engineering.

I later married the man of my dreams when I came back home to attend my grandmother's funeral. He was watching me the whole while I was in the church. When the funeral was over, he walked over and introduced himself to me. He was tall, handsome and very cute. He said he was a builder of custom homes and tree houses. We dated for a short while and soon got married; everyone attended the wedding because we were both from the same place. His name was Mr. Willie Anderson but most everyone else just called him *Bug*. We nick-named our first daughter *Cutie-Bug* and as soon as she was old enough to know better, we built her a gigantic pink tree house in our backyard – not too far from the first pink tree house ever in our town.

# THE CEREAL MURDERS

I always thought it was funny how children and adults could occupy the same planet but live in different worlds at the same time. One Saturday morning long ago, my brother Tyrone and I anxiously sat at our breakfast table, waiting for Mom to pour our favorite cereals. I liked Frosted Flakes, and he liked Sugar Pops; I was nine, and Tyrone was two years older than me. We were fidgety because as soon as we finished our breakfast, Mom was driving us to the neighborhood Boys Club to meet up with the other boys and the camp leaders. We were going to spend the weekend camping at Camp Lakey. This would be our first ever overnight camping trip away from home and the comforts we knew.

Behind our mom's back during breakfast, we sometimes combined our two favorite cereals, and my brother and I would race to see who could eat the most cereal – with and without milk. Sometimes we ate so much we threw up. We always had cereal for breakfast while Mom and Dad ate stuff like grits, bacon and eggs. Yuck! There was nothing sweet about any of that stuff. Mom said all the sugar we ate made us hyper and rambunctious, especially when she caught Tyrone and me fighting over the empty cereal boxes. Cereal boxes were neat; we used the boxes to make cool things like toys, games, and anything else we could dream up. I once made a real-looking pirate hat out of my box. Tyrone turned his box into a shoe and clogged around, pretending to be a wounded soldier with a club foot. We even made miniature suitcases out of our cereal boxes in case we ever decided to run away from home. At our ages, our imaginations were limitless.

"Tyrone, Dexter, time to go. Let's load up," yelled Mom.

"All right, Mom," we both yelled back as we jumped up from the table, leaving our empty cereal bowls and grabbing our gear and backpacks.

The drive to the club was only a few miles, but as Mom was maneuvering the car in the front seat, we were horsing around in the back seat. Tyrone unzipped my backpack on purpose and made my stuff drop out. While I was bending over picking up my stuff off the floor, he pinched my butt and made me yelp. In turn, I untied his sneakers and then stuck my fingers in his ears. He hated when I did that. When he tried to cover up his ears, I would tickle his underarms, making him scream in agony.

"Boys, that's enough. Thank God we're here," Mom said as she abruptly stopped the car in front of the club. Mr. Alford, one of our camp leaders, was standing out front waiting for us.

"C'mon boys, the others are waiting in the van. We need to get going. We still have to get there and set up camp," said Mr. Alford as he waved us out of the car and waved bye to Mom with the same hand.

We each quickly kissed Mom, jumped out of our car, ran around the back of the building, and jumped into the Boys Club van. In all, there were twelve boys in the van ranging from ages eight to twelve. There were also three other camp leaders in addition to Mr. Alford. Mr. Hawk, Mr. Bell, and Mr. Fordham were each along to make sure we behaved and didn't get out of control; Mr. Fordham drove the van because he was more familiar with the directions to the camp. He told us he had first gone to Camp Lakey when he was a kid many, many years ago.

The drive to the camp was very rural but scenic. During the drive, we stared out the windows and pointed at the many cows, horses, cotton fields, cars, houses, and trees along the way. We also drank plenty of cans of soda, sang loud songs, and secretly threw spitballs at each other. In about an hour or so, we pulled into the gate at Camp Lakewood, the real name of the campground, but everyone just called it Camp Lakey. The campgrounds were very well kept and known to be a natural habitat for deer, foxes, owls, eagles, raccoons, opossums, skunks, and other neat animals to see. No one had ever mentioned snakes, so we did not expect to see any.

As soon as the van stopped, Mr. Alford told everyone to take a quick bathroom break and meet back at the van so we could start setting up our pup tents. We scampered out to the bathroom to relieve ourselves of all the soda we had consumed. Each of the pup tents was only big enough to sleep about two or three boys. Of course, I had planned to bunk with my brother. When we got back to the van, Mr. Bell had the rolled-up tents laid out on the ground. He made us line up and come and get our tents when he called our names.

"Bernard and Wendell, take this tent and set it up over there by that tree," Mr. Bell commanded. "Bay-Bay and Moon-Eyes, you put yours up near that other tree." Mr. Bell used the nickname for these two brothers because that's what everyone always called them. Bay-Bay was probably a slang version of Baby, but it was quite clear why Moon-Eyes got his nickname. This kid had the biggest eyes I ever saw. He always looked scared, like his eyes were going to pop out. Moon-Eyes also was known to have a big appetite.

"Tyrone and Dexter will set up on the other side of those two tents." It went like that until the tents were passed out; each camp leader helped supervise the setting up of the tents by helping us dig the holes for the tent poles. After we were finished with the tent setup, we had to search the grounds for wood so we could make fires during the night. We planned to use the fires for keeping warm and for cooking too, since there were no nearby stores. Mr. Hawk was known to be a good cook, and he specialized in grilling steaks, hotdogs, hamburgers, and barbecued chicken. When Mr. Hawk wasn't serving as a volunteer camp leader and cooking on his grill, he was an undertaker at the local funeral home.

Now that the tents were set up and the wood was gathered and stored, we were allowed to go swimming in the lake until Mr. Hawk was through fixing our food. The lake was warm and mainly shallow – not much danger of us drowning. Besides, each of us was a good swimmer, but Tyrone was probably the best swimmer. The dinner bell rang out just as we were getting tired of splashing, diving, and doing backflips in the water. We quickly dried off and ran to stand in line. When it was my turn in line, Mr. Hawk filled my paper plate with a hotdog, a hamburger, a drumstick, baked beans, and potato salad. An ice chest full of canned sodas like Mountain Dew, Coke, and Dr Pepper sat nearby, and we each grabbed our favorite ones. I gave my potato salad and baked beans to Moon-Eyes, but I ate the rest. While we ate our special food, Mr. Hawk served steak to himself and the other camp leaders. Mr. Bell, a large man with a big belly, said he liked to eat his steak rare, but I did not understand what he meant back then.

When we finished eating, we chucked our paper plates in the trash and begged to go hiking down a nearby nature trail. Mr. Alford led the way as we whistled and marveled at the new and unusual sights we saw and sounds we heard in the woods. We saw robins, blue jays, and sparrows. Overhead, we spotted two eagles perch in a tree, then majestically soar high above the trees and clouds. As we walked on, we saw two raccoons chasing each other and three deer drinking water from a pond. After about two hours of sightseeing, we began to feel tired, so we turned around and hiked back toward our campsite. When we returned to camp, the sun had gone down, and we were hungry again. Luckily, Mr. Hawk had anticipated that and had our food ready. It was leftovers, but it still tasted great. This time, I even tried some baked beans and potato salad, and I had three cans of Mountain Dew.

As soon as we finished eating, laughing, and joking around, the camp leaders announced it was time to turn in for the night since we had a full day of activities. But we started to protest by saying, "No, we're not ready to go to sleep yet. Tell us some ghost stories."

"Ghost stories?" asked Mr. Alford.

"Yeah, my dad said they always roasted marshmallows and told ghost stories when he went camping as a kid," said Wendell. "And we want some ghost stories, but I don't like marshmallows."

"But I don't know any ghost stories I can tell," said Mr. Alford, looking puzzled. We started booing and crying, "We want ghost stories, we want ghost stories, we want ghost...."

"I've got a story I can tell, but it's not a ghost story," interrupted Mr. Fordham with a weird smile. "It's about something terrible that happened not far from here, but it might be too much for you boys."

"Please tell us anyway. We want to hear it, please. We're not scaredy cats," we yelled.

Mr. Fordham looked around at the other camp leaders to get their approval. At first, Mr. Alford objected by saying, "John, I don't think you should tell that story to these young boys." We booed and continued to boo until Mr. Alford relented. Mr. Fordham again looked at the other camp leaders, and they each nodded affirmatively. Then he looked at us and asked us if we were sure. Of course, we said yes in unison. Then he said, "Okay, gather around the campfire, and I'll get started. But make sure you sit close to each other and hold on tight to your blankets because this is a true story. This is a story about the serial murders that happened many years ago in Headland about a mile or two from here."

"Cereal murders?" I asked.

"Yes, serial murders committed by real serial killers," Mr. Fordham continued. With my mouth wide open, I looked at Tyrone and he looked back at me, both of us thinking the same thing. We looked around at the other boys, and everyone looked scared already, especially Moon-Eyes.

"The serial killers were three brothers who murdered nine innocent people. They were the Hillsman brothers, and their names were Dwight, Rudy, and Henry. They each looked just alike, and most people say they were triplets. They were big, bald-headed and ugly. They broke into their victims' homes and first ate their food. Then they took their personal belongings, including their pet dogs, cats and goldfish. Finally, they killed everyone in the house by chopping off their heads," Mr. Fordham whispered as he grabbed a long piece of firewood, raised it high above his head and then came down real hard like he was using an axe. We jumped when he did that and covered our eyes with our hands.

"But what happened to the cereal..." I tried to ask, but he interrupted my question.

"Oh, the serial killers did get caught, but it was long after they had committed their deeds. As a matter of fact, they buried some of the heads of their victims in the woods. That's why it's called Headland today."

We shrieked as Mr. Fordham pointed toward the woods, his eyes now as big as Moon-Eyes'. Just then, we heard a strange sound from the direction Mr. Fordham was pointing. It did not sound like any of the sounds we had heard when we were in the woods earlier. The sound got louder and louder, as if the thing was crawling toward our camp. Suddenly the fire startled us when it crackled loudly as some of the burning wood began to shift because of the hot flames. We began to snuggle closer together while looking around for each other to make sure we were all still there. Mr. Bell, who was eating his second plate of meat, stood and peered out over the woods to see if he could see anything. When the noise stopped, he sat back down, gnawed at his bloody steak, and continued listening to Mr. Hawk.

"Probably just an owl or a wild hog," he said as he licked his fingers.

"What happened next with the cereal killers?" Tyrone asked, anxious to hear more but still looking scared at the same time. I kicked Tyrone under our blanket to make him shut up, but I was too late because Mr. Fordham started up again with his scary story.

"When the police finally caught the serial killers, they tried them in court and found them guilty; they then sentenced them to death. To be sure, they put stakes in their hearts, cut off their heads and buried them in the woods with their victims – and there was no coffin. Some people say at night, you can still hear all the amputated heads talking and whispering to each other asking, 'Where is my body? Where is my coffin?'"

"Please stop. We don't want to hear anymore. That's enough!" we cried.

"But I haven't gotten to the best part yet. Are you sure you want me to stop?"

"Yes, please stop. We're ready to turn in now."

"I think that's enough, John. Let's let them go to sleep," Mr. Alford said.

"Okay, boys, I think that's it for now. We can finish the story tomorrow, if you like," teased Mr. Fordham.

"No, thank you," we said together.

Each group quickly disappeared into their assigned pup tents. Tyrone and I raced to our tent and jumped into our sleeping bags. We got very close and held onto each other real tight.

"Tyrone, you think the cereal murderers will get us?"

"No, because we don't have any cereal with us, Dexter," he said, sounding unsure of his answer.

I didn't think of that, and it initially made sense to me. But I still didn't get much sleep because I heard the creepy night sounds coming from the woods. I really believed it was possible for the cereal murderers to kill us, so I dared not close my eyes. Every sound made me wince and jump. I couldn't wait until daylight.

We heard a loud howl and a rustling sound coming from outside our tent that made both of us sit up straight in our sleeping bags. Suddenly, Bay-Bay and Moon-Eyes scurried into our tent and asked if they could sleep with us. Before we could answer, they had crammed in and huddled next to us, saying they were scared; they were shaking, and so were we.

"Did y'all hear Mr. Hawk say they cut off their heads?" asked Moon-Eyes.

"Yeah, and he said the heads weren't coughin' when they cut them off," added Bay-Bay.

I looked at Tyrone and said, "That's right. Mr. Hawk said the heads weren't coughin' but they could be heard whispering, 'Where is my body? Where is my coughin'?'"

"He also said they put steaks in their hearts. Why'd they put steaks in their hearts?" asked Moon-Eyes.

"I don't know," said Tyrone. "Maybe somebody wanted to eat the bodies of the cereal killers, too."

When Tyrone said that, I thought of Mr. Bell gnawing on his steak and licking his fingers as I envisioned the killers' bodies being eaten. The others must have had the same vision because we held onto each other tightly and dared not go to sleep. We now planned to stay up all night on our first-ever overnight camping trip away from home and the comforts we knew.

"I got to pee, but I'm too scared to go to the bathroom," Bay-Bay said. "I think I had too many sodas."

"You can't go out there. Something might get you in the dark," said Moon-Eyes as he looked at me and Tyrone to get us to agree.

"Will one of you go with me?" asked Bay-Bay.

I realized I'd had too many sodas and needed to pee too, but I didn't want to go outside either, especially with Bay-Bay, who was only eight. I said, "I'll go with you if Tyrone goes with me."

"I don't have to pee, and I don't want to go outside," said Tyrone. "Why don't you look around for something to pee in, so you don't have to go outside?"

We used a flashlight to search around the tent. All we found were a few empty Mountain Dew cans. "I found two cans. Here Bay-

Bay, you take one, and I'll take the other," I said as I passed one of the cans to him.

Bay-Bay took the can, unzipped his pants and tried to pee into the can. He missed the tiny can opening in the dark and peed all over our sleeping bags. Tyrone yelled, "Bay-Bay!"

"Sorry, I missed! It's dark in here."

By the sound of it, Bay-Bay filled his Mountain Dew can to the brim. After it was all full, he tossed it outside our tent. Next, I unzipped my pants and tried to pee into the can without missing the hole. I found the opening, but I had so much soda in me, the can spilled over from too much pee and further wet our sleeping bags. We had to smell pee the rest of the night, and there was definitely no going to sleep now.

"You think the cereal killers are going to get us tonight?" Bay-Bay asked.

"Tyrone said no because we don't have any cereal with us," I said.

"Me and Bay-Bay like Fruit Loops. We eat them all the time at home, but not anymore," said Moon-Eyes. "I'm too scared to eat them now."

"I used to like Frosted Flakes, and Tyrone used to eat Sugar Pops."

For the rest of the night, we kept talking like that to keep each other awake, reminding ourselves that we did not want to be victims of the cereal murderers at Camp Lakey.

The next morning was Sunday. We peeped out of the tent and found the campground quiet again. The sun was shining, and Mr. Hawk was yelling that breakfast was ready. When we got dressed and reported for breakfast, we saw plenty of paper bowls, plastic spoons, milk cartons, and boxes of cereal: Frosted Flakes, Sugar Pops, and Fruit Loops. We just stared in astonishment, and nobody made a move toward the cereal, not even Moon-Eyes.

"What's the matter?" asked Mr. Hawk. "Y'all want something else? I got some left-over steaks if you want that instead."

Mr. Hawk and the rest of the camp leaders seemed genuinely shocked when we said we weren't hungry and just wanted to go home. The men looked at each other, scratched their heads, and finally, Mr. Alford said, "Okay, let's load up and get out of here."

We hurriedly rolled up our tents, gathered our stuff, and headed toward the van without waiting for our camp leader's permission; we were clearly ready to leave Camp Lakey and get back to our homes and our parents. I guess we wanted to be sure the cereal murderers didn't get to them while we were gone. On the way back home, we were as quiet as could be. No loud songs. No spitballs. No horseplay.

Because we got back sooner than expected, Mr. Hawk dropped each of us off at our respective homes. When we got to our house, Tyrone and I jumped out of the van as soon as we could without even saying goodbye; Mr. Alford must have thought we were crazy. We rushed into our house and immediately started calling out for Mom and Dad. Dad was sitting at the kitchen table, and Mom was getting ready to make breakfast. Tyrone and I rushed over to each one and gave them a big, long hug.

"What are you boys doing back so early? We didn't expect to see you until this evening. We thought you were going to spend the whole weekend there," Mom said.

"Uhhh, we missed you and wanted to make sure you were all right," Tyrone said.

"Yeah, Mom, we missed you and Dad," I added.

Mothers know when things are not right, but our mom didn't push the issue. She looked at Dad and decided to table the issue for then, knowing she would get to the truth later. "How 'bout something to eat? I was just going to make your dad some steak and eggs. I've got your favorite cereals."

As Mom walked toward the pantry to grab the cereal boxes, I looked at Tyrone and he looked at me. Before she could open the door to the pantry, I said, "Mom, we want pancakes!"

"Pancakes? I thought you guys only liked cereal. You never wanted pancakes before," she said as she stopped in her tracks.

"We wanted to try something new. We learned that at camp," Tyrone said.

"Yeah, we learned that at camp," I echoed.

"We also learned that eating steak and eggs is bad for you," Tyrone said as he looked at Dad.

Mom rolled her eyes and looked at both of us, trying to figure out if we were for real. She looked over at Dad and then she said, "Okay, pancakes it is."

Dad, looking disappointed because he had his heart set on steak and eggs, gave in and said, "Yeah, pancakes would be nice for a change. I can do pancakes."

A little while later, Tyrone and I sat at our kitchen table with two large pancakes each on our plates. We watched Dad slather butter on his pancakes and then pour syrup over them. Mom, noticing the frowns on our faces, told us if we didn't want syrup, we could also use honey or molasses. She got up from the table and brought back the honey and the molasses and set them on the table next to the syrup. I looked at Tyrone and he looked at me. It seemed we were both thinking the same thing. First, we used some of the syrup, then some of the honey, and then some of the molasses. Then we raced to see who could eat the most before we threw up. From that day forward or until we learned better, we never ate another bowl of cereal for fear that the cereal murderers would come and kill us.

# A BIBLE FOR UNCLE BOBBY

My Uncle Bobby used to be a record-spinning disc jockey in the mid-'70s. He definitely had music in his bones as he was forever the DJ at all the house parties; he even made a business out of playing records for parties, weddings, and funerals, too, if they let him. Uncle Bobby seemed to have every record by every R&B artist that ever existed, especially all the popular artists of the day like The Temptations, The Manhattans, Earth, Wind & Fire, The Delfonics, Al Green, and of course The Godfather of Soul, James Brown. He even liked the smell of the vinyl records – both the 45s and the albums – and could always be seen reading the liner notes on the backs of the albums and answering trivia questions about the artists.

When the new and improved compact discs replaced vinyl records in the '80s, we thought for sure Uncle Bobby would die, but he didn't – he adapted; quickly, too, I might add. He started storing all his CDs in zippered leather cases, which was much easier than carting around crates of albums in the trunk of his car. Everyone in the family just figured Uncle Bobby would be playing music forever. When he got older, Uncle Bobby made a remarkable change. To everyone's surprise, he became an old-fashioned, fire-breathing preacher. No more booty-shaking, devil-worshiping music for him – he was strictly all about the Lord, and he was not playing with God or in it for the money. Uncle Bobby was sincere, and the change that came over him was real.

My grandmother was so impressed with Uncle Bobby's change that she bought him a new Bible. It was one of those large, heavy

Bibles that was encased in a leather case and had a zipper. They came in brown and black; she got him a black one. Uncle Bobby was proud of that Bible, and he took it everywhere. When he felt he had read and understood most of its contents, he asked Reverend Ingram if he could maybe preach a trial sermon at our church, The Open Bible Baptist Church. In the South, a trial sermon is like a practice sermon for a new preacher; it lets him get up in front of a real congregation and see if he has what it takes to be a preacher and then a pastor one day.

Reverend Ingram graciously agreed to let Uncle Bobby preach his trial sermon at our church, and they set a date for him to deliver it on the fourth Sunday. The word quickly got out in the community, and people were more anxious to see the miracle of my uncle's conversion than they were to hear what he was going to preach about. Of course, there were some naysayers in the community who only believed he was in it for the money, but others were genuinely in his corner. Mrs. Grace, our next-door neighbor, actually went out and bought a new dress for the occasion. She said she'd known my uncle since he was a baby; she wanted to look good on the day he preached his first sermon. Mrs. Grace said God got the jump on the devil by snatching my uncle into the church before it was too late. She said it was only right for her to dress up for God on Sundays and wish my uncle well at the same time.

The fourth Sunday had finally come, and Uncle Bobby was raring to go. We watched him dress up in his best black suit, white shirt, and thin black tie. When he was finished, he looked just like a preacher. We all hurried out the door to get to the church because we wanted to get there on time. As we all piled into Uncle Bobby's car, he said he was so nervous he forgot his Bible. He asked me to run back inside and get it. I ran back inside, saw the black leather Bible on top of the stereo, grabbed it, and ran back to the car.

It was a beautiful Sunday for a trial sermon. The Open Bible Baptist Church choir had all its members present, and they all wore beautiful blue robes. The church was packed, and Reverend Ingram even let Uncle Bobby sit up in the pulpit next to him. Uncle Bobby sat there beaming as he clutched his black leather Bible. Reverend Ingram said he was proud to be able to introduce Uncle Bobby on this special day. After the choir sang a beautiful hymn, Reverend Ingram got up and gave a nice introduction to Uncle Bobby. He said, "I have watched this young man grow up in the church and in the community. I am very proud to have him here today. After the choir sings one more song, the next voice you hear will be the voice of Mr. Bobby Seawright." The church applauded as Reverend Ingram sat down, and the choir stood up to sing.

While the choir sang, Uncle Bobby unzipped his black leather Bible to brush up on his sermon. He had written his sermon the night before and stored a copy inside his Bible. When he opened it up, he realized that a terrible mistake had been made. Instead of having his Bible, he was holding one of his leather CD cases filled with CDs. I had inadvertently picked up the wrong leather case and handed it to him. Unbeknownst to the rest of us watching, Uncle Bobby was scared. He slowly got up and walked to the podium after the choir finished singing. He looked out onto the congregation and said, "Good morning, church." Everyone said good morning back in return. He said, "Amen and God is good." In plain view of all of us watching, he then looked down at his open Bible as if he were reading from it and said, "The subject of my sermon is *Ain't Too Proud to Beg* because He is the *Sunshine of My Life*." The church clapped and said, "Amen."

Uncle Bobby continued reading and preaching from his Bible by asking, "Is it *Just My Imagination* running away with me or are we living in a *Ball of Confusion*? *People Get Ready* because a train is coming. *Ain't No Mountain High Enough* and ain't no valley low enough to keep us from God. Today *I Feel Good* because I'm standing on the *Good Foot*. James Brown said, *I Don't Need Nobody to Give Me*

*Nothing, Just Open Up the Door and I'll Get it Myself.*" The church gave thunderous applause and urged him to continue.

Uncle Bobby said, "*The World is a Ghetto* and you need *Devotion* to *Keep Your Heads to the Sky. Ain't No Use in Worrying* because you can always *Lean on Me* and I'll be your *Bridge over Troubled Water.* If *Nobody Wants You When You're Down and Out*, then *You've Got a Friend* in me. *Beauty's Only Skin Deep*, but if you just *Check Out Your Mind*, you'll see that you don't want to be on that *Midnight Train to Georgia,* but you do want to climb that *Stairway to Heaven* in *The Midnight Hour.*" Everyone in the church stood on their feet and clapped. Then Uncle Bobby closed his Bible and walked out in front of the podium empty-handed, but he continued to preach.

"With God, you found *Love on a Two-Way Street* and His love is an *Expressway to Your Heart. What Does It Take* to win his love? *What's Love Got to Do with It?* You know *Still Waters Run Deep,* but God wants to ask *How Deep Is Your Love?* On that great day, there's going to be *Dancing in the Street* in Heaven, but it's going to be a *Heatwave* in hell. I'm asking you to *Rock Steady* and hold onto God's hands as tight as you can."

Uncle Bobby went on like that for about twenty-five minutes. He must have gone through every song on every CD in his case, but nobody seemed to mind. When he finished, his face was soaking wet with sweat; the church gave an overwhelming nod that he had done a good job on his trial sermon. Of course, later on we found out about the mistake with the misplaced Bible. Uncle Bobby said he wasn't worried because God had put the words before him, and he was only doing God's will. Now every time I hear one of those old songs like Al Green's "*Love and Happiness*" or The Delfonics' "*Didn't I Blow Your Mind This Time,*" I smile and think of Uncle Bobby's sermon.

# VIDALIA

I fell deeply in love with Vidalia when I was fifteen years old. To set the record straight, this story concerns two Vidalias. The first Vidalia is the name of my hometown city located in Toombs County, Georgia, which was incorporated in 1890. Like several other towns, Vidalia was raised around a rusty railroad yard that primarily catered to nearby farmers who grew such vital crops as tobacco and pecans; however, Vidalia became more famously known for its sweet onions, popularly named Vidalia onions. But that was not the Vidalia that I loved or the one that stole my heart in 1947.

Vidalia Jemison was the beautiful fifteen-year-old Georgia girl who stopped me in my tracks when I first saw her. There was no wonder why her parents named her Vidalia. She had a pecan-colored complexion, long, curly pigtails, and to me, her bottom was shaped just like a sweet Vidalia onion. She was my first love. It was true that her family was part of the many tobacco farmers, but she never smelled like tobacco to me; my family cultivated land to grow pecan trees, and we didn't smell like pecans.

Vidalia was the oldest of three girls in her family and the prettiest to me. Valerie was eleven and Vivacious was thirteen. I could feel that Vidalia liked me a lot, too. In school, we would sit and stare at each other from across the room. When the teacher would call on us, we would become embarrassed because our minds were too fixated on each other to answer. After school, I would always walk her home and take the shortcut through the pecan orchards. When the leaves were full on the large trees, they provided a good cover for what I had planned in my head. Once we got into the orchard thicket where no one else could see us, I stopped and lightly kissed her Georgia peach lips. Vidalia looked at me intently with her dark brown eyes, dropped her books and pulled me in closer for a longer, deeper kiss. Then she said, "Emory Higgins, I was wondering how long it was going to take you to kiss me." Thereafter, we took the shortcut through the pecan orchards every day that school was in session, and we always stopped in the thicket. It was too bad we didn't have school all year round back then.

Mr. Farby Jemison, Vidalia's father, was considered an important man, primarily among the Negro families. His family had been farming tobacco for years, and their knowledge and skill were well known. He employed many of the Negro men in town except for those who worked for my dad in the pecan industry. Mr. Jemison understood the significance and perils of raising three young brown-skinned daughters in the South; he wanted to make sure they got a good education and then moved away from our town that did not offer them much if they stayed. His wife, Ophelia Jemison, made sure to teach each daughter how to cook, sew, iron, and how to use proper ladylike etiquette when out in public. In spite of all that, I often chuckled to myself when I remembered the time Vidalia threw her books and her etiquette away to grab me and kiss me. Although we never actually discussed marriage, we both wanted the same thing and couldn't wait to move away to some bigger city to be together. I wanted Vidalia to be my wife with all my heart because there was no other girl for me in my future. However, my future with Vidalia would not come to pass after what I later learned from her sisters.

When school was out, Vidalia and her sisters would often ride with their father to the railroad yard near town to deliver his loads of cured tobacco leaves to the trains. It was his way of teaching them about the business world and letting them see the town at the same time. He made Valerie and Vivacious stay near the wagon while he took Vidalia inside with him to conduct his business; he would often pay some of the Negro men standing around to unload the tobacco from the wagon. The railroad yard was always bustling with a lot of activity due to all the different farmers trying to get their goods to market.

On the way out of the business office with her father, Vidalia inadvertently stepped on a piece of wood with a nail in it; the nail went through her shoe into the bottom of her foot. She fell to the ground in pain, and her father saw the nail sticking in her shoe. He quickly pulled the nail out of her shoe and noted that it was a rusty nail. Realizing that he would not be able to take Vidalia to a doctor in town, he put her on the wagon and rode the ten miles back home to let his wife take a look at her foot to see what she could do.

Once they made it back home, Valerie ran inside to get her mother. Vidalia was crying hard from the pain, but mainly because she was scared. Mrs. Jemison knew that stepping on a rusty nail was not a good thing and that she needed to act quickly before infection set in. She looked around in her kitchen for some fresh raw meat to apply to the wound in order to draw out the poison. Although she preferred a good piece of steak or a pork chop, she settled for three fat strips of cured bacon that she wrapped around Vidalia's foot with a white piece of cloth and an apron string. She gave her some aspirin for the pain and then put her to bed so that her foot could rest. There were no Negro doctors around, and the White doctors in town would not think of treating a Negro girl even if her life might depend on it.

After three days with a very high fever, Vidalia's condition did not improve at all. Her normally small foot, still swollen from the nail, was almost twice its size now. In desperation, Mr. Jemison rode into town to beg the town doctor to try to help his daughter. The doctor, who knew Mr. Jemison quite well, hemmed and hawed until he announced that he had just been called out to deliver a baby from a nearby neighbor. The doctor suggested he take Vidalia to the local Negro midwife who was well known for delivering babies, not mending feet.

Mr. Jemison galloped back home as fast as he could to be with his oldest daughter in her time of need. As he approached the porch, he heard the loud cries coming from his wife and daughters. He rushed through the door to see a white sheet pulled over the body of my future wife, Vidalia. His wife said that about an hour after he left, Vidalia started convulsing, screaming, and talking out of her head. The last thing she said before she died was "tell Emory I love him."

When the news got to me from her sisters, I was speechless. All my dreams and plans of marrying Vidalia were gone in a flash. Immediately, I thought about quitting school and running away from Vidalia, Georgia, for good. There was nothing there to make me stay. I loved my mom and dad, but not like I loved Vidalia Jemison.

During her funeral, I walked up to her casket and kissed her hand in front of everyone. I left the church before the burial because I could not stand to see her casket placed into the ground.

Vidalia died fifteen years ago at age fifteen. Today I am thirty, and I have never married. I probably never will because Vidalia Jemison was my soulmate and the only girl ever for me.

# IT'S COMPLICATED

Love can sometimes be complicated, like E=mc², Einstein's Theory of Relativity. It's befitting that the analogy of this complex mathematical equation with love is just as appropriate and relevant as Newton's scientific law on gravity: "What goes up must come down."

If magnets seem rather bipolar, that's because they are. But people are not supposed to be bipolar or confused, especially when it comes to love. When it comes to love (and lust), it seems that humans are governed by three major laws: God's law, man's law, and Mother Nature's law – also known as natural law. God's law is easy to understand as the Bible speaks out against lust and infidelity. Man's laws against infractions of love and crimes of passion are usually dealt with in courts. Yet Mother Nature seems to supersede both of these laws when it comes to love or lust – she makes it very complicated and does not follow a black-and-white rule in determining what's right and what's wrong. She tempts the heart and the mind to believe and manifest the literal translation of Einstein's Theory of Relativity – "energy equals mass multiplied by the speed of light squared" – to mean that the urgency of love or lust felt must be dealt with head-on, regardless of which laws are to be broken or violated. Nestor Perlongher, a great poet, once wrote: "We do not want respect, we want to be desired." Take the following case in point:

My college roommate, Anthony, was in love with his girlfriend Jacqui, and they had planned to get married right after graduation. They dated the whole four years we were in school and had become soulmates, it seems. Everyone who saw them knew they were in love

162

and that they were meant for each other. Anthony once told me Jacqui completed him like no other woman he had ever known. She completed his sentences, read his mind, and every time she touched him, it felt like a warm fire. Of course, I was jealous because I had never experienced anyone or anything like that before. I mean, we were both barely in our twenties, but Anthony had beaten me to the punch when it came to love.

True to their promise to each other, Anthony and Jacqui did get married after college. I was his best man, and I witnessed the most beautiful wedding ceremony I had ever seen. A few years later, Anthony Jr. came along and soon after that, a girl named Norah. Anthony and Jacqui had made a wonderful family, and the whole world was at their feet. Still, I was single and yet to find that special lady. I dated a lot, but the one I was expecting had not shown up with my glass shoe.

Year seven of their marriage, Anthony called me and invited me out to a bar to have a drink. I didn't think anything of it because we routinely got together for drinks, although it had been a while. But this time was different. I immediately noticed that Anthony seemed a little off-kilter, not himself. At first, I tried to ignore it and wait him out; I figured he would tell me sooner or later. Anthony began to drink more and talk less so I broke the ice.

"Hey Ant, what's up? You seem different tonight. Everything okay?"

"I don't know man, I'm confused."

"I can see that. How can I help?"

"You can't. I love Jacqui with all my heart. But..."

"But what, man? I know you love Jacqui. I've been a witness to that for the last seven years. There are no buts. Whatever you're thinking...."

"I met someone...someone else."

"Someone else? What are you talking about? An affair?"

"Well, I didn't mean to. I mean, I wasn't looking for...."

"Whoa, man. What are you saying? You can't have an affair with anybody else. Think about Ant Jr. and Norah."

"I am thinking about them. That's why I'm here with you now trying to sort this out. You are my best friend, right?"

Anthony then looked up at me, and I saw a look in his eyes I had never seen before. He was scared, but it was a different kind of fright. Not like he was afraid to die but more like he was afraid to live. Between the two of us, Anthony had always been the more level-headed. I could sometimes be wild and illogical, but not him. Realizing this was much more than I realized, I decided to take a different, non-judgmental approach. I relaxed, ordered another round of drinks for us and said, "Tell me about her."

"Jacqui?"

"No, the other one. What's her name?"

"Synthia."

"Synthia, huh? That's a pretty name. How'd you meet her?"

"She works at an office building next door to mine and we sometimes run into each other at the food court. We usually smile when we see each other, and one day we just said hello. We introduced ourselves and just happened to sit at the same table for lunch. It was no big deal."

"What happened next?"

"Nothing, really. Over the next few weeks, we'd find ourselves in the food court at the same time, and it started to feel familiar; you know, kind of nice."

"She must be very pretty."

"Yes, she is, but that's not what first attracted me to her."

"It's not? Then what was it?"

"Her touch. When we shook hands."

"What? Her touch? Didn't you once tell me that when Jacqui touched you it felt like a warm fire or something like that?"

"Yes, that's right, but Synthia's touch is different."

"How so?"

Anthony stopped for a minute to think. Then he looked at me and smiled.

"The only way I can describe it is like this: I now know how Benjamin Franklin felt when he was struck by lightning while holding a kite in the rain."

"Wow!"

That was about all I could say. I didn't know how to respond because I was still single and had no reference for being struck by lightning. Again, I was jealous or envious of Anthony due to his life-altering experiences that I could not understand.

"Have you guys ever...."

"Made love? Yes. And it was like nothing I've ever experienced before. Being with Synthia is other-worldly."

"Wow! I don't know what to say. But I thought Jacqui was your soul mate."

"Did you ever think that maybe it's possible to have more than one soul mate? I don't know. All I know is what I feel for Synthia is real and does not feel like lust. I also love Jacqui with all my heart; I would never want to hurt her or the kids in any way. They can't know about this. I've got to find a way to figure out this whole thing."

"Don't worry, brother. I won't mention anything to anyone about this, but you've got to get some professional help. Maybe see a marriage counselor or something."

"Yeah, that's a good idea, but I don't know, man. What am I going to do? I can't have my cake and eat it too."

"No, you can't," I said with no judgment.

We continued drinking for another hour, and then we left without saying another word about it. We hugged each other and parted ways.

Over the next few days, I did not hear anything else from Anthony. I prayed that he had taken my advice, things had worked out, and he was in a better place. I dared not call the house because I did not want to be questioned by Jacqui.

A week went by, and I ran into another friend named Nathan at the grocery store.

"Hey man, are you still close friends with Anthony?"

"Yeah, why do you ask?"

"I just heard that he and Jacqui are having troubles in paradise," said Nathan.

"Why would you say that, man?"

"Because Jacqui and the kids moved in with her parents and Anthony is not with them," said Nathan.

"Damn! What? I did not know that."

"I'm just saying, man, that's what the word is. Sorry."

I left the store and went straight to Anthony's house. I knocked on the door, but no one came to the door.

As I walked off the porch, a police car drove up and stopped in front of me.

"Are you Anthony Franklin?" asked the policeman.

"No sir, I'm his best friend, Raymond Kelly. I was just checking to see if he was home."

"We received a 911 call that there was some type of emergency at this address," replied the officer.

"I know where they keep the spare key, Officer, if you need to go in and check things out," I said while thinking the worst-case scenario.

I located the spare key, and the officer and I went in. When we got to Anthony's bedroom, we found him lying on the bed with what looked like a self-inflicted gunshot wound to his head.

The officer looked at me and asked if I knew any details about what may have led to this.

All I could do was drop my head and tell the officer, "It's complicated."

# MAMA DOODLE'S PORCH

Living in the South wasn't always as turbulent as it's normally portrayed. Yes, there were plenty of hard times and days where life was not optimal, but I have fond memories of the times when life was simple and good in our neighborhood. One of my most favorite memories is sitting on Mama Doodle's porch listening to various townspeople tell stories. We delighted in drinking iced tea with lemons and mint julep leaves, and eating homemade gingerbread cookies. Sometimes, we had popcorn too.

Mama Doodle was not a relative but she was one of the most beloved residents in our close-knit community. She lived alone but never complained about being lonely. She was in her early 90's but still spry and fiery. People often said they would see this little old lady doodling around in her yard planting flowers, or doodling in her rocking chair, going back and forth while shelling peas or shucking corn. Mama Doodle might also be singing church songs in a high-pitched voice, which was a funny sight to see since she was not a songstress. Everyone started calling her Mama Doodle and she didn't seem to mind because she knew it was an affectionate title. Her porch was always open and welcome to anyone who wanted to stop by and sit for a spell.

She had been a widow ever since her husband passed away in the 1940s. People said he was kicked in the head by their mule named Buster and he never recovered. Mama Doodle's real name was Mrs. Pensy Mae Coleman and her late husband was Mr. Othel Coleman. They got married when they were very young and had never been apart until his death. They were unable to have any children but she claimed all the neighborhood kids as her own; likewise, all the children loved Mama Doodle.

Mama Doodle lived in a quaint wooden house with a screened-in porch to keep out pesky mosquitos, flies, wasps and bees during the hot southern summers. Many people complained about being eaten alive by mosquitos or bitten by bees or wasps back then; most people screened in their porches but sometimes those flying bloodsuckers managed to get inside and wreak havoc on everyone.

I recall one special summer evening when several of us kids and a few adults sat around on Mama Doodle's porch laughing and telling funny stories that nobody really believed but we told them anyway. One of the funniest local tales was about Mr. Hawkins, the neighborhood funeral home owner. Mr. Slew Lou Walker, one of the adults sitting on the porch, told the story about the time when Hawkins Funeral Home was called to pick up the corpse of a man who had been pronounced dead by his family. When Mr. Hawkins took the body out of his hearse and placed it on the embalming table, he realized the man was not actually dead yet. Looking around to make sure no one saw him, Mr. Hawkins picked up a hammer and hastened to finish the job so that he could get paid for his funeral services. Although people laughed heartily at the story, they still tip-toed and walked hurriedly by whenever they passed Hawkins Funeral Home.

Another funny story was told by Mr. Penny Mavis. Mr. Mavis could spin more yarns than any five people and he never seemed to run out of tales. It was said that Mr. Mavis never let the truth stand in the way of a good lie, but he could always be heard exclaiming, "I ain't lying!" Mr. Mavis, now a hog farmer, said he was a cook in the army back in the day but not a very good one. He said he recently cooked some fried chicken and tried to feed some to his hogs but they refused to eat it and ran the other way. His prize hog was named Ruth. He yelled, "Ruth, you better come back here and eat some of this good fried chicken!" Ruth reportedly turned around and said, "Penny, I'd rather eat slop than eat your fried chicken." After watching everyone fall down laughing so hard at his yarn, Mr. Mavis loudly proclaimed, "I ain't lying!"

Next Mama Doodle told a story about picking cotton when she was a young girl. She said she picked a huge burlap bag of cotton that took her all day long and only got paid about eighteen cents. She said in order to make more money, she started putting rocks in the bottom of the sack. She then told us the most she ever made was thirty-five cents for the whole day. We young people howled and really got a kick out of imagining Mama Doodle as a little girl; we realized that she was almost 100 years old.

Deacon Harry Wright started a story about seeing a ghost in an abandoned old church when he was a boy. He said he and two friends were walking by the church one evening at dusk and heard a weird howling noise inside. They peeked through one of the windows and saw what they claim was a ghost. When asked how he knew it was really a ghost, Deacon Wright was quickly interrupted by Mr. Mavis, saying "Excuse me Deacon but I got a better story than that. It's a real hum-dinger and I ain't lying."

Mr. Mavis jumped up and said, "My Uncle Chinch Chambers was an automotive genius who bootlegged liquor for years and never got caught!"

Mr. Mavis continued, "Uncle Chinch installed a double-barreled gas tank on his old pick-up truck to haul the moonshine. When he got stopped by the liquor police, they could never figure out where he was hiding the moonshine. One time one of the young coppers got wise and guessed that Uncle Chinch was hiding the liquor in his gas tank. The officer was so sure he was right, he siphoned some of the contents from the gas tank and poured it in his coffee cup. When he put the cup to his lips to drink, he quickly discovered it was gasoline and dumped it on the ground. The police were dumbfounded but they had to let Uncle Chinch go."

Mr. Mavis laughed really loud and said, "If the cops would have known Uncle Chinch had a second gas tank full of liquor, they would have put him under the jailhouse."

Everyone roared after hearing the tall tale, including Deacon Wright. For the next hour, Mr. Mavis told tale after tale until our parents called us to come home to eat dinner. I always smile when I think of those easy times when we were all brought together by simple story-telling with a few cookies, iced tea and popcorn.

A few years later Mama Doodle passed away from natural causes. On the same day as her funeral, a small tornado hit town and demolished Mama Doodle's old wooden house. The concrete porch slab was all that was left standing as everything else was destroyed. After that several people in the neighborhood said they walked by the old home site and heard what they said sounded like a high-pitched voiced singing a church song; most attributed what they heard to the high winds left over from the tornado.

A year after Mama Doodle died, Mr. Mavis passed away too. The story was he was feeding his hogs one day and dropped dead near the hog pen. When they found his body, his prize hog Ruth was by his side snorting while the others stood by and kept a protective watch until help arrived. It was reported that Ruth said, "Penny must have died from eating his own cooking."

"I ain't lying!"

# "1ST KISS"

First kisses, like first loves, have a way of staying with you forever. Of course, I have to separate all the other kisses you get from your mother, sister, aunt, and other female relatives from that special kiss you get from that special girl.

Before I became the great kissing machine that I am now, I had great teachers or role models to learn from when it came to knowing how to kiss a girl. I watched all the great male kissers on television and saw how they made girls swoon during a hot and steamy kiss. These real men types fueled my imagination with enough electricity to light up a nuclear power plant. With my kissing skills firmly intact from watching years of television, I was ready to burn that special girl's lips right off her face.

I vividly remember the first time I kissed a girl, although I was not sure she felt the same way. I was in the 9th grade and I knew I had found the love of my life. I quickly went from cowboys to girls and was feeling my oats. Finding my girl coincided with the release of Stevie Wonder's "My Cherie Amour" because her named sounded similar. We talked on the phone every night for hours but not really saying anything except for,

"Whatcha doing?"

"Nothing. What you doing?"

"Nothing."

And it would go back and forth like that for hours. I hadn't learned how to cut through the chase and just tell her what I really wanted to say. She was being very coy too or she hadn't learned much either since she was a 9th grader also; however, girls do mature faster than boys. In her defense, girls back then were taught to exercise a lot of restraint and weren't that aggressive. They were being lady-like and would often leave it up to the boys to make the first move. I didn't have very many moves and I wasn't sure how and when to use the one move that I thought I had.

I asked permission from her parents to take her to a movie, and they agreed as long as we returned home before dark. Of course, I was not old enough to drive so we had to walk downtown to the movies. The movie theater was not that far and walking gave me a chance to build up my courage and act like I knew what I was doing. I walked on the outside of the sidewalk and let her walk on the inside like I saw the real men do on television.

Luckily, we found a matinee showing around 3pm. For that showtime, we could take our time walking home and still get back way before dark. After paying for the movies, I purchased a box of popcorn, two drinks, and a Nestle Crunch chocolate bar just in case she wanted something else sweet.

We both wore sneakers, T-shirts, and starched, white denim jeans which were the rage back then. After the movie, we walked home slowly; we held hands all the way and told each other how much we really enjoyed the movie and each other's company.

I got close enough to smell her and smiled when I thought she smelled good just for me. The sun was still shining and it made her face light up even more when she smiled back at me. I knew she was the only girl for me and that she would be mine forever. Her white teeth sparkled and her long hair blew in the wind as we turned the corner to her house.

We had never kissed before but I felt tonight would definitely be the night I got my first kiss. It was an expensive special night on the town for us. My weekly allowance was blown after the movie, the popcorn, drinks, and candy bar; all that had set me back about five dollars. I kept the chocolate bar in my shirt pocket, hoping to eat it on my way home. I then reached into my jeans and pulled out a lone stick of Juicy Fruit gum; I took half and gave her the other so that our breaths would be fresh when we kissed.

When we reached her home, we notified her parents that we were back before dark and would sit on the porch swing for a little before I headed home. Her mother smiled and her father gave me a look that said, "Good thing you made it back before dark because I was ready to come looking for you!"

I could tell her mother liked me, but I was never sure about her father. Maybe he was just being over protective or something. We then went onto the porch and sat on the swing, still holding hands. The sun started to set as we finished talking about the movie and other small talk. Then when it was dark enough that no one could really see us, we both got quiet and stared in each other's eyes. We instinctively knew that the magic moment we had waited for had arrived. The moon was shining bright and all the stars had lined up in the sky to say, "This is it! What are you waiting for?"

Just when we both closed our eyes and leaned in to kiss, her little sister ran out on the porch and jumped in my lap. It startled me at first because I thought it may have been her father pulling us apart.

The little sister stayed just long enough to overstay her welcome with me. Quickly, I thought of a way to get rid of her so we could finish the kiss we started. I reached in my pocket and gave the little sister the chocolate bar. It was soft and beginning to melt and I was hoping she would just take it and go, but she didn't. She actually opened up the paper, grabbed the chocolate with her hands and sat back down in my lap. Then she put her hands on my thighs and got chocolate all over my white jeans.

I shrieked and her mother ran out from the noise and grabbed the little sister saying, "Child, come in here and leave them alone!" Her mother apologized and left to give us some privacy. She must have realized how important first kisses are and what they mean to young people. I could tell her mother had once looked just like the girl I had fallen in love with.

I looked down at my jeans and saw chocolate stains all over them. When my girl saw how dismayed I was, she said, "Let's finish what we started" to get my mind off my messed-up jeans. Without taking any chances or waiting any longer, we moved back in to touch lips but our eye glasses got in the way. We each took off our glasses and tried it again. Our foreheads bumped this time as we tried to get too close too fast. Next our teeth clashed because we both opened our mouths at the same time. After several awkward and unsuccessful attempts to actually connect and kiss, she pecked me on the cheek and offered to walk me outside, sensing she had better go inside before her father came to get her. But I was not yet defeated. I was even willing to face her father's wrath by overstaying my welcome to get my first kiss.

We walked outside in the moonlight holding hands tighter than ever. When she was just about to say goodnight, I surprised her by perfectly kissing her lips like I had seen done many times before on TV. First, my heart stopped and I heard soft music playing in my head; then my heart started beating faster than ever before.

The sweet smell of her got all over me and my clothes as she firmly embraced me and softly kissed me back. Our passion consumed us and our souls seemed to intermingle inside our bodies for a second. Although my eyes were closed, I sensed someone looking at us through the porch window. I slowly opened my eyes to see that it was her father. He watched his daughter hold me tight and whisper, "I love you so much" to me. Without saying a word, he quickly disappeared from view. He also turned the porch light on to indicate her time was up and she had better come inside now. I took that to mean he was beginning to like me or that he was unwilling to embarrass his daughter at a time like this.

I skipped on air all the way home, and said, "Thank you" over and over to my TV teachers. I knew I was different then and would never be the same again. How would I be able to describe my first kiss to my friends? Or should I not kiss and tell and just keep it confidential between me and my girl? Either way I had passed the test of a good kisser but so had she. My heart couldn't keep quiet and was beating like a drum; my lips felt as smooth as silk but cool like Jell-O. I couldn't wait for my second kiss.

The next week at school girls smiled at me as they passed by in the halls. I sensed that they knew something by the way they acted. I felt I was getting way more attention than I deserved. Even some of my teachers commented that I had a new air of confidence about me and wanted to know why. I just smiled and said, "I must be maturing a little."

When I saw my girl later on that day, she had a special glow about her. Her teeth seemed whiter, her hair seemed prettier, and she smelled even better than I had remembered. I asked her what made her so different and she just smiled and said, "Well, I had a date over the weekend and got my first real kiss. It was so unforgettable that I just had to tell my friends. The first boy I ever kissed was you. I can't wait for our second kiss."

I grabbed her hand and walked her to class beaming with the biggest smile ever on my face. It seemed our first kiss was unforgettable for both of us after all. Many more kisses followed after that but none could compare to that first kiss; it was magical and it transformed both of us.

# Bonus Writings

retrieved from my literary archives also known as
"Paper Orphans"

These bonus writings do not just rely on my imagination, but are part of our collective reality. I hope that these last few words resonate with you and explain why I added them as a bonus and adopted them for publication in this new volume.

"I often write creatively to remind
myself I am still alive."
– James L. Thompson, Jr.

# "THE THUMB SUCKERS"

I am a thumb sucker. I was born a thumb sucker and all through grade school, I sucked my thumbs. When I got older, I graduated from Thumb Suckers University where I majored in… well, you already know.

I am not alone though. There are millions of us out there. People who suck their thumbs are normal just like everyone else. As a baby, I sucked my thumbs and tucked my ear lobes inside my ear so I could go to sleep. I dreamed that my thumb was a big lollipop in all different flavors; it was the best pacifier a baby could have.

I had the cleanest thumbs in my family. My parents tried putting pepper and vinegar on my thumbs to stop me from sucking them, but I was too far gone. I stuck them in ketchup or mustard and kept on sucking.

Several girls and boys in my neighborhood were also thumb suckers, but some were too ashamed to admit it. I was proud of my thumb-sucking skills so I organized an unofficial thumb sucking club called The Thumb Suckers. At the height, we had over 15 boys and girls in our club who sucked their thumbs on a regular basis. We all took a thumb sucking oath to suck our thumbs whenever we wanted to without fear or shame.

Sucking my thumbs only came to a halt when I found an abandoned puppy. I loved this little puppy so much and wanted to care for it all the time. My parents only let me keep it unless I agreed to clean up after it. I eagerly jumped to the task by first giving my puppy a name. I named him Scruffy because he reminded me of a shaggy stuffed toy dog.

Scruffy followed me everywhere and even slept with me in my bed. I fed him scraps of food from my own plate because I didn't know what else to feed it. He liked fresh water but he didn't go for milk; he also liked popcorn and peanuts.

Early one morning I awoke after I smelled something awful coming from my bed. Looking over at Scruffy, I figured out that the smell was coming from him. I quickly checked my sheets and saw a big blob of puppy poop; I knew my folks would kill me if I didn't clean this up in a hurry. I grabbed an old newspaper and used that to clean the poop off the bed. When I went to throw the paper away, I got puppy poop all over my hands, especially my thumbs. I washed my hands but I could still smell the poop on them. I washed them again but the smell was still there.

The next day I called a meeting of The Thumb Suckers to tell them about what happened. I remember Fat Jerry saying, "Oooh, I know you're not going to suck your thumbs anymore after that." I looked dumbfounded and said, "Well, I guess I can't anymore now."

That was the last time The Thumb Suckers ever met. It seems that my story about Scruffy served as a deterrent and stopped everyone else from sucking their thumbs. Who knew it was that easy?

At church a few years ago, I saw a six-year-old boy sitting with his parents and sucking his thumb. I looked at him and commented, "Wow, I used to be a thumb sucker too. But I quit a long time ago."

The parents looked at me in amazement. They were looking for a way to stop their son from sucking his thumb. They asked how old was I when I stopped sucking my thumb. I looked at them and winked my eye, "Well, I'm 60 years old now and I stopped sucking my thumb about a week ago."

The boy instantly took his thumb out of his mouth. His mother looked at him and said, "Now see Tommy, you don't want to still be sucking your thumb when you're 60 years old like this man, do you?"

Tommy stared at me and didn't say a word. For added effect, I stuck my thumb in my mouth and sucked it right in front of him.

The next time I saw his parents they thanked me and said I scared Tommy so bad that he quit sucking his thumb immediately. They added, "But he since started this weird habit of tucking his ear lobes in his ear to go to sleep." I smiled and said, "I can't help you with that."

# "SHELF LIFE"

We recently had a food drive at our church and asked people to bring canned goods to give to the needy. The local Boys Club Troup brought in thousands of donated canned goods, and they also helped to organize the cans by their dates.

While sorting, we noticed that some of the cans had surpassed their Expiration Dates and their Best Used By Date by several years. Due to liability laws, we could not afford to give those expired cans to the families and had to throw them away. We spent the whole day sorting the cans and finally were able to provide the families with the food donated to help sustain their lives.

Afterwards, I thought about how a human's life is like a canned good that's pre-packaged and stamped from inception. It's funny to say but the similarities between human beings and canned goods like sardines or green beans are uncanny.

We humans also have a shelf life with Expiration and Best Used By Dates. The Best Used By Date is merely a suggestion to do so before it is too late. When Benjamin Franklin said, "Don't put off until tomorrow what you can do today" he was talking about our Best Used By Date. Saving money for a rainy day does no good if you live where it rains all the time. The contents are best consumed in time.

Expiration Date means the choice has already been made and it is terminal. Surely, none of us plan to live forever, but we can all plan to live life the best we can before we are taken off the shelf.

I once heard two men argue about life and death. One said that the worst thing for him was to get old and die. The other countered by saying that the worst thing for him was to get old and not be able to die. The latter felt that being kept alive against his will was a far worst fate than dying, for he longed to see his heavenly home. That exchange permanently changed the way I looked at life and death.

Butterflies are some of God's most beautiful creations; however, the average lifespan for a butterfly is just two to four weeks. Imagine how a butterfly must feel starting out as a caterpillar and then earning its wings to fly away toward the heavens. A Mayfly has the shortest lifespan of any living animal on our planet. The adult lifespan from this particular species is only 24 hours. Knowing these things allow us to fully appreciate our lengthy human lifespans.

Contrary to popular belief, a cat does not really have nine lives and a rabbit's foot is not really lucky. Maybe these are just old fantasy tales to make us feel more human. In the end, be careful to view the dates on the canned sardines you are about to consume. If the dates are several years old, you may affect your own shelf life.

# "REPEATING RIFLES"

The ghost of Alabama's late iconic Governor George C. Wallace lives deep within the hearts and souls of some modern-day governors like the current Florida GOP Governor. This governor has emerged as a frontrunner in the 2024 race for the U.S. presidency. Many of his sordid motives and talking points come straight from past playbooks; he is both a disciple of #45 and an heir apparent to his narcissistic lunacy. All these men were acting like repeating rifles often shooting at the same old targets.

The statement, "Those that fail to learn from history are doomed to repeat it" has been attributed to several past philosophers, including Winston Churchill. However, we can all agree that lessons from the past may not actually predict or ward off doom, but they can provide insights into the reminiscent present and possibly even the grave future when it comes to a candidate vying for the presidency of the United States of America.

The political landscape and diverse political ideals of America have changed tremendously since the days of George Wallace and Winston Churchill. The idea of forming a more perfect union today in the U. S. amidst all the premeditated chaos is akin to swimming in shark-infested waters with bloody underwear; it is guaranteed to cause continuous bites in the rear from all directions.

The Florida governor harbors and generates more homophobic and racial manure than anyone could imagine from a person living in our futuristic times. He is truly a relic of the past who unearthed himself and is simultaneously unearthing fears and hatreds long since thought buried in America.

A repeating rifle is a single-barreled rifle capable of repeated discharges between each ammunition reloads. Speculation runs rife that this governor is both a repeating rifle and a metaphoric arms dealer in hatred disguised as a prolific patriot. Every time he shoots off his mouth, he leaves tons of political carnage behind that make it difficult to see a victorious end for him. Banning African American education from Florida schools is an example of the latest hard-to-believe things he has done. While citing the reason that a course in African American studies has no educational value, he has blatantly insulted a race of people who literally built this country with their blood, sweat and tears. If he wins the 2024 presidency he will be known as an "AK-47" to represent the 47th President of the U.S.

Ignoring and attacking the LBGTQ community is another tactic the governor is continuously involved in executing. His absurd "Don't Say Gay" policies are both incredulous and immoral. His attack on the Disney Corporation has been a media nightmare for the state of Florida, and one that is destined to backfire as it proceeds. Disney has always been viewed as a welcomed home to all people regardless of race or gender.

It is difficult to understand how a political candidate can expect to win any political race by equally alienating voters who identify as Black and/or LBGTQ. Time will tell if this repeating rifle's political strategy will afford him the leading position that he craves in winning the U.S. presidency. Time will also record the history of the many current affairs involving race and gender that are still contrary to us being one nation under God, indivisible, with liberty and justice for all.

# "A BUTTERFLY'S WINGS"

Butterflies don't start out with wings
They acquire them through a transition
As caterpillars, they tread and toil the earth
In a humble fashion until they earn such things

Although every butterfly was a caterpillar,
Not all caterpillars become butterflies
If a caterpillar is not patient, faithful, and strong
Somewhere along the transition her dream dies

The wings of butterflies are outwardly
They are the dreams come true of optimistic worms
Like getting a second chance in a new life
The caterpillars are reincarnated but on new terms

They now happily use their wings to symbolize
The rewards that hard work and faith bring
And how God replenishes the humble
And blesses the butterfly to sing

No better creature is there
Than the blessed butterfly
To teach us about life on earth
And life beyond the sky

# "SAFETY NET"

Like a safety net,
I'll always catch you if you fall
and I know you'll also catch me

In the politics of love,
You'll always vote for me
and I'll always vote for you

As long as our hearts share the same platform,
Our love will always be in office.
In this life,
We always need someone to catch us
because falling is a part of being human

Falling becomes less fatal when
someone is there to catch us

Safety nets and politics are the same
When it comes to love

You'll always catch me when I fall
And you know I'll also catch you

# "LOVE IS LIKE GLASS SLIPPERS"

When Prince Charming presented Cinderella with the glass slippers,
he symbolically placed his heart in her hands.
Fragile, rare, and crystal clear,
the glass slippers perfectly reflected his love.
The light that sparkled so brightly through the slippers
was only matched by the light that sparkled in her eyes
when she first saw them.
For in that moment, Cinderella knew the value
of what the prince had given her.
When she eagerly slid her feet inside the slippers
and found a perfect fit, it felt like magic.
And so is it with love and friendship alike.
It is equally rare to find someone with whom we click.
But when we do click with someone, we find that the
friendship is both delicate and crystal clear.
As magical as it may seem, we'll never be the same again.
In love and in life,
when you find a shoe that fits,
simply wear it.

# "WATERFALL"

With every single drop
I stop
To reflect on what you
Meant to me and how I
Wish you would have stayed.

Your calls turned into
Letters and your letters
Turned into notes,
Reminding me not to forget you
With love.

My mind remembers well
And so does my heart;

My eyes are ever-flowing
And the water will not stop.

Is there any way at all
To cushion my water's fall?

# "MEN WHO CRY"

Men who cry
must have hearts made of sponges;
men who don't
must have hearts made of stone.

Men who cry
display an uninhibited courage
to feel compassion and empathy
for human frailties.

Men who don't shed tears
were cast in that prehistoric mold
set eons ago by those who lie
and by those who are near-extinct.

Men who cry
reveal a God-given emotion
which separates them from inhuman creatures
who lack the ability to show sorrow.

Men who cry
can hear the cries of other men
and make them know it's
natural to taste the tears of heaven.

Men who cry
are men like me.
I am a man who cries
and feels for love and friendship.

Men who cry
are men of a chosen lot.
as we cry, we will inherit the wind
to gently blow away our tears.

# THE 23RD PSALM

The Lord is my shepherd; I shall not want.

2 He maketh me to lie down in green pastures: he leadeth me beside the still waters.

3 He restoreth my soul: he leadeth me in the paths of righteousness for his name's sake.

4 Yea, though I walk through the valley of the shadow of death, I will fear no evil: for thou art with me; thy rod and thy staff they comfort me.

5 Thou preparest a table before me in the presence of mine enemies: thou anointest my head with oil; my cup runneth over.

6 Surely goodness and mercy shall follow me all the days of my life: and I will dwell in the house of the Lord forever.